ALLURE

of *the*

MAIDEN

BY R. C. WAGNER L.

ISBN: 0692896368 (Paperback)

ISBN: 978-0692896365 (Paperback)

DESERVED RECOGNITION

It would be an undisguised lack of gratefulness if I did not acknowledge the contribution of my faithful companion and friend, my wife Lian, in having allowed me the time taken from associating with her to write this book. May there come to be a perfect wage for her.

All references to individual characters or places made mention of in this publication are fictional. Any comparisons to persons living or dead, or to specific locations where events may have transpired, are opinions held by the individual reader of this literary work and not necessarily those of the author.

TABLE OF CONTENTS

One- ARRIVAL IN SAN JUAN

Two- THE DIARY

Three- REASON FOR THE VISIT

Four- A PRICE TO PAY

Five- NO TIME TO LOOSE

Six- THE HOSPITAL

Seven- ALFONSO'S

Eight- THE CAPTAIN OF *LA DONCELLA*

Nine- LEFT BEHIND

Ten- THE TALE

Eleven- THE DILEMMA

Twelve- THE UNWILLING PARTNER

Thirteen- ESCAPE BY SEA

Fourteen- THE COLONEL

Fifteen- THE ISLAND OF *EL PINO*

Sixteen- ROUTE TO THE NORTH

Seventeen THE FINAL REWARD

Eighteen- A LESSON LEARNED

Chapter 1

Arrival in San Juan

T he sun was gaining strength for another day as it challenged the last vestige of the night. The shadows were receding, losing their battle to the increasing light of the morning. The humidity and its inseparable partner the heat were making their daily climb from hot to unbearable. Another day had begun, and the streets were alive with activity even at this early hour.

As Bill threaded his way amongst the people and stalls in the street market, he came across men bent into submission by the loads on their backs, as well as women who strode with decisive steps transporting large vegetable laden baskets on their heads. People were crossing the streets, scurrying about. Some were dodging the few cars or trucks driven with no thought of others. Everyone was trying to arrive and attend to matters of the day, and all who met up with him acknowledged his presence with their eyes. A group of teenage girls dressed in their customary school uniform found him more than curious, and worthy of extended consideration.

The inn where he had passed the night wasn't far from his goal, which was arriving at the train station on time. Still, it took longer than he thought to walk the distance. His pace had been slower than normal since the night hadn't been as kind as he had wished. The bed was short, narrow, and the sheet the same. He had passed a good part of the night occupying himself with swatting mosquitoes, listening to their annoying high-pitched sound. It was not the best situation for a restful sleep. He had managed though to get up and put things in order for this final leg of the journey.

About half way through the street market he came to the corner where he needed to turn. As he rounded the corner the train came into view. A worn wire fence vainly attempted to separate the activity of the street from that on the station's wood platform.

Finding the station located on the West side of town was accomplished without much difficulty. On the taxi trip from the airport the day before he had seen the train station, and he made a mental note of where it was located. However, some of the details were rather vague due to the hour of the day and his having slept poorly. He managed though to not get lost, or end up on a street where his wallet would have more value than his life.

Pausing momentarily, Bill took in the scene while adjusting his backpack. On the station platform merchandise was stacked haphazardly, waiting to find its place on the train. The passengers who had not as of yet climbed onboard were milling about, displaying mixed emotions with taking the final step to leave town. Their ambivalence stemmed from feelings of sadness in leaving friends behind, while at the same time family called them home. Others were aware that arriving home would mean being in the company of those whom they did not consider to be friends, and for this reason they were in no hurry to leave town. His attitude however, was one of expectancy of things hoped for.

Seeing the train gave him a flush of emotional buoyancy.

Attentively considering the train from a distance, he could see that it was a steam locomotive. It was linked to seven passenger cars that were apparently veterans of many years of service. None of the equipment had received much upkeep, only what was absolutely necessary. The cars had been painted green at some time in the past. Now, however, the wood was showing through in several places. The windows were equal size squares without glass. There was practicality in this, seeing that discarding unwanted objects was infinitely easier.

That fact became apparent when a banana peel was flung from one of the windows, narrowly missing his head. The woman responsible offered no apology; she simply looked with a measure of curiosity at the foreigner. Her large jowls moved slowly, reducing the banana to pulp. Then a long laborious swallow aided its descent.

He continued on, wiping the sweat from his brow. Momentarily distracted with this mopping action he bumped into one of the passengers also traveling to San Juan. The collision prompted Bill's apology.

"Sorry about that." There was no verbal reply from the other party, just a slight nod of the head.

Approaching one of the cars he took hold of the handrail and placed a foot on the first well-used metal step. Then, he climbed up onto the landing. Accomplishing this, he carefully maneuvered his backpack through the door trying to not catch it on anything. A heavy breath escaped his lips as he slipped it off and placed it on one of the wood benches that served as seating. The noise from the backpack landing on the wood bench startled some chickens resting at the feet of one of the passengers. The clucking hens with tied legs soon continued their conversation amongst themselves with descending volume.

The passengers had arrived early, which was always a good idea. No one knew exactly the hour of departure. More or less it would leave about 7:00 a.m. It all depended on the activity of the preceding night. Namely, if the conductor of the train could get himself together, clearing his head of the beastly abuse that he had forced on his body with company of questionable character at one of the local *cantinas*.

In the distance to the right of the train, the mountains rose abruptly from the alluvial plain where pineapples ruled the cultivated fields. One of the summits, *La Bonita*, was catching the early morning sun and clothing the rainforest on its slopes with an iridescent green. Its peak swaddled by mist was not to be seen.

The tranquility of the moment was stopped abruptly by a child's voice.

"Fish! Fried fish!" His eyes changed from the mountains to a young boy who stood in the aisle.

"You want some fried fish *Señor*?"

The boy was not alone. Five companions also formed part of this troop of upcoming merchants. All of them were wearing stained and ragged shirts, as well as shorts in the same condition. The shorts lacked little from coming to rest around their feet.

Bill looked the group over with an amiable expression. After closer inspection, considering the state of the fish, he shook his head and politely said no. They definitely had been fried, yet, when this had taken place was debatable.

The fish boy removed the bowl from underneath his nose, which gave space for another of the young vendors to thrust some bags of dried papaya and corn meal muffins at him. They also were refused. Others on the train indulged themselves with the products offered.

This commerce continued until a blast of the whistle scattered the vendors and notified all that the train was about to leave. Today the trip was starting fifteen minutes early; the unexpected was to be expected.

The seven cars with their collection of people, goods, and animals began to move. The engine shook and belched thick, black smoke. He watched from the window feeling that an explosion could be in the making as the train labored with its load. After an apprehensive and doubtful beginning the ride began to smooth out. He could sense a constant forward movement with a subtle swaying from side to side. As the steel wheels gathered momentum turning faster and faster they lost the shrill squeaks that had characterized their initial revolutions. They began to harmonize into a steady sound with the increasing speed of the train.

The wind coming through the windows produced a delicious sensation as it pressed the sweat-dampened shirt against his body. The same breeze also cleared the air of the smells that had begun to accumulate inside the car.

Leaving town was not a long drawn out affair, as there was a definite point where the town stopped and the countryside began. The train moved along, the scenes changing from marshy meadows that surrounded groves of dense jungle growth, to areas where fields of heavy grass and Ceiba trees extended out to reach the descending slopes of the mountains. Some trees were laden with moss. So much so that they gave the impression that they were melting. A sudden gust of wind and the moss would transform itself into hundreds of refined ladies dancing gracefully in long flowing skirts.

There were few amenities on board. However, the conveyance did afford freedom and time to ponder on the beauty that flooded through the windows.

The clicking of the wheels as they passed over the seams of the rails marked time, just as the movement of the hands of a clock. There was an unending uniformity with a somewhat narcotic effect, to which he succumbed. A numbed sleep came upon him making the trip shorter than it was. Periodically jolts of movement, or a crying baby would summon him back to consciousness. In this half awake mental state the details of that day when he found the diary at his father's house would intermingle with other thoughts. Abruptly, such pleasant memories were stopped by the loud cries of someone.

"Hey, stop the train! Hey, can't you hear? Stop!"

The passengers came out of the lethargy that had engulfed them. A man outside, on top of one of the cars was shouting at the conductor to stop. The reason was one of the passenger cars had uncoupled coming to rest a distance back down the tracks. When the conductor finally heard the shouting he applied the brakes, slowly, nothing must be done hurriedly since it wasn't his fault. The sound of metal to metal, the punctuated collision of car-to-car and then, the train stopped. With an accompanying shudder and groan it started in reverse to find the orphaned child it had left behind.

Wondering what was taking place, Bill slid his backpack to one side and moved closer to the window where he could see what was happening. A thought came to him. Possibly the proceedings could be better appreciated from the back of the car where a more complete picture was to be enjoyed. No one else in the car seemed to be particularly interested in all of this. In fact, their expressions indicated that they considered the matter an uneventful episode in another prosaic day of life.

From the rear door he could see five people in the abandoned car with either their heads protruding from the windows, or resting their elbows on the window frames. They were occupied with looking into the distance at the mountains or scenery in general, waiting with stoic dignity, knowing that sooner or later the car would be missed.

The train moved closer and slowed its approach. He moved back inside, not that he doubted the ability of the conductor, but he didn't wish to experience the error of his confidence either. There was a sudden jolt, the joining of hitches, and this time, a closer inspection of the necessary items. As all was apparently in order the call was given to start out again.

Finding his seat, he scattered a few eyes that had taken to looking at him with curiosity. All that was required was that he stare back at them, their timidity did the rest.

Settling into his seat while the train continued with its task of transporting passengers and freight, he attempted to rest his head against the side of the car, calmly watching the passing scenery. There was abundant plant life, as well as the fleeting final movements of animals that lost themselves searching out where to hide amongst the plants. Some bickering sea birds revealed how close the rails followed the shoreline. At selected moments he could see the water through the groves of coconut palms and jungle growth, making a stark contrast between the deep green of vegetation, and the shades of blue that danced across the surface of the sea.

The morning marched towards midday, the heat being briefly punctuated at intervals by the shade of plants forming a tunnel around the tracks. He actually felt somewhat comfortable. The smell of the sea mingled with the warmth of the wood bench. The sounds around him became muffled. The pains of his disgruntled body from the lack of sleep faded, and his thinking began to blur between reality and dreams. He began to enter and exit periods of much needed sleep.

In this state, his mouth opened slightly, allowing a bit of saliva to run across his chin. He continued oblivious to this condition until his sleep was again interrupted by the train's whistle. They were approaching San Juan, and the entire village was being called to action for this highlight of the week.

Sitting upright, clearing his throat and trying to focus his eyes on the scene ahead, he could see children and dogs flowing towards the train like a marauding hoard set for the attack.

There were individuals present with obvious reasons, and others with an unknown purpose. A man loaded down with plastic cups, containers, and other trivia prized by women of these parts. There was a farmer sitting on burlap bags of dried cacao beans, waiting to sell his crop to one of the merchants who traveled the line.

Nicolás was also present, expecting some items being sent to him on the train. Bill hadn't experienced the displeasure of knowing Nicolás yet. He would learn though that Nicolás was not one to be numbered amongst your friends.

Children and women climbed the ladders of the train, pushing their way through those trying to exit. The air filled to capacity with their voices calling out what it was they had for sale. They begged the interest of the passengers for the fish, or fruit that they carried in an assortment of baskets. It meant a great deal to find buyers.

Bill's body had stiffened somewhat, so he stood, stretched well, and then took hold of his backpack. He shouldered and secured the load, then gave a glance at the seat and under it, to see if by chance he was forgetting something.

Maneuvering his way through the train he came up against a rather bulky woman. Due to her size she never worried about the lack of padding on the benches. With consideration for propriety, he tried to get around her, which was not an easy task.

Outside the sun was shining brightly, marking definitely where it gave way to the shade. Squinting, he tried to get his bearings tipping his hat so as to afford the best protection possible for his eyes.

He saw the local store, which in the past had been a well-stocked commissary of the fruit company, and considered it to be the best place to start his inquiries.

People in places like San Juan know all their neighbors. Unfortunately, they know everything about their neighbors as well.

Not yet noticed by him, many pairs of eyes were already scanning the stranger.

As he came closer to the store two small boys approached him.

"Good-day." They bowed and folded their hands in front of themselves in a gesture of prayer.

Bill gathered that they had mistaken him for a priest, most of them being like himself a foreigner. They would periodically make an appearance in the village to attend to the parishioners and collect what funds were available. The two boys ran off hurriedly after this social obligation of respect, kicking an old can that served as a ball.

The store, which belonged to Nicolás, resembled a train car with a porch and windows. The structure stood about three feet off of the ground, with the main floor joists resting on posts that had been driven into the sandy soil. Being elevated above ground level provided for circulation of the air, thus avoiding the wood-rot, mold, and decay that objects were subject to in the tropics.

Two men leaning against the railings of the store porch took note of Bill's approach. Their furtive glances came to an end when he smiled. Prompting them to hide themselves behind tilted beer bottles, which they accomplished with an air of indifference towards the stranger.

As a young man Nicolás had worked for the fruit company. When the company left the area he acquired a sizable amount of land, but more through artful contrivance than hard work.

He enjoyed the respect, or so he thought, of those who lived in San Juan. They sought him out when they really needed something. This dependence of others upon him made him feel indispensable. How he relished it when they would come to grovel at his feet for the favor of a loan, a little help in some way, an unexpected emergency that only he could resolve. In his own eyes he was so important.

At times this self-coronation as a man of social stature made it awkward for him to abide by basic decency. According to Nicolás, what was good for him was the proper course to take, irrespective of how it affected others.

"Hello." Bill scanned the items that sat on the shelves as he waited for an answer.

A curtain over the entrance to the back of the store parted slowly. Inés, Nicolás' wife made her entrance.

Her steps were measured, her gait that of self imposed dignity. Head high, she gave a condescending look at the stranger. Suspended by a thick gold chain around her corpulent neck was the medallion of a favorite saint. Her regal aspirations were betrayed by the soiled and disheveled dress that stretched itself out over her abundant body. Nothing more than her blue rubber sandals separated her from the earth.

"Hi, I want to know if you could give me some information. I am looking for Jorge Valladares. He lives here in San Juan. Do you know where he lives?" Inés considered the question. She moved closer and rested her arms on the counter. He could see the beads of sweat trapped in the fine black hairs of her upper lip.

"What did you say?" Though she had heard perfectly well the question, it was in her nature to exact all the information she could from petitioners.

"I am looking for Jorge Valladares. Do you know where his house is located? I know he lives here in San Juan, but I am not familiar with the area." Inés interrupted;

"You are a *gringo*, aren't you? But, you speak pretty good Spanish." Bill actually spoke excellent Spanish, but Inés couldn't bring herself to see merit or abilities in others. For her, 'it was pretty good'.

Returning to his question, Bill again inquired as to Jorge Valladares. A somewhat cynical smile masked her face.

"Does he owe you money, is that why you are looking for him?"

"No. He is a friend. Can you tell me where he lives?" The restless night had produced a somewhat sharpened edge on his tongue, and she was capable of bringing out the worst in anyone.

Inés came out from behind the counter and walked with laborious indifference towards one of the windows. She lifted her arm to point, allowing the folds of flesh between her elbow and armpit to drape unhindered.

"You follow the road across the tracks and then up the hill. When you come to the school, Jorge's house is right beside it. After a slight pause she allowed herself a final acerbic verbal assault.

"Friends usually know where each other live."

Bill was undecided if he should laugh at the women or not. Being a stranger he withheld what he was desirous of saying.

"Thanks, I appreciate the information." As he turned to leave some jars of mint candies on the counter caught his attention. "How much are the mints?"

"You can have five for twenty *centavos*."

"I'll take ten of them, please."

Inés took hold of the jar with her plump fingers. A cockroach that was hiding between the jars scurried across the counter. The mints and the money exchanged hands. Bill thanked her before turning to continue on his way.

She moved to a window placing her elbows on the sill. From this perch she followed the stranger with her eyes. There was nothing but questions that flooded her mind.

On the porch, one of the two men in an expression of intelligence belched. Through the window he handed her the empty beer bottle, which she accepted reluctantly. Directing his comments to her but following Bill with his eyes, he asked in a questioned affirmation.

"He said he was looking for Jorge?"

She said nothing. Her head moved to the side so as to look at the man with a mixed look of displeasure and disbelief. He dropped his vision from Bill and meekly directed his vision at the ground.

"Do you have problems with your hearing? You have been standing right there. You heard everything he said." Cowered by the reply the man looked away.

The three continued watching as the foreigner followed the directions he had been given.

It was a short distance to Jorge's house, made even shorter by his mind being occupied with the expectancy of meeting his father's former work companion.

The Sandy road was kicking up little dust as he walked along. Palm trees and leafy plants along the way provided shade. Hardly any birds were to be seen flying. Their calls revealed where they hid amongst the vegetation, away from the brunt of the sun.

San Juan was a desirable place to live from the viewpoint of one who loves nature. The hushed natural sounds of an agrarian community accompanied by the muted sound of waves rolling up onto the nearby beach. Life was guided by the cycle of day and night, planting season and harvest.

He came to the point where a small stream cut across the road. A peaceful stream now, but one that in the rainy season gave birth to a torrent of muddy waters carrying plant life towards the sea. At this time of the year it could be easily crossed without wetting your feet, if the right stones were chosen. As he walked he kept his eyes opened for the school, enjoying the tranquility of the moment.

The road started up a gentle incline and then turned towards the left. It passed an abandoned adobe church.

On the right side of the road was the school. It was a long building as buildings go in San Juan, and it obviously was very old and in poor repair. On the side that faced the road there was a covered porch, which ran down the entire length of the building. Protected by the porch roof there were two doors located one at each end of the covered entrance. Between these doors a continuous opening of about four feet covered by wire mesh ran the entire length of the building itself, allowing for air movement. In front of the school an old bell hung from a beam, now scarcely supported by two posts. In the past it had been used to call the children to classes.

The school had been a busy center of learning when the fruit company had drawn many families to the area. Now, however, it had lapsed into an understaffed and underfunded excuse for educating the few children of the village who could afford books, paper, pencils and other items that were to be provided by the students.

Having arrived at the school, his landmark, he muttered to himself.

"Well, this must be it. That house right over there is probably the one."

He approached the door and knocked. There was a feeling of apprehension as to how he would be received.

A young girl of around eight years old opened the door slightly. She peered through the opening, the sunlight highlighting her face against the dark interior of the house. She stood in silence considering the stranger.

"Hello. Does Jorge Valladares live here?" She said nothing. Abruptly, the door closed in his face. She then ran to the back of the house and Bill could hear her excited declaration...

"Papá, Papá. There is a *gringo* at the door and he said your name." A deep voice, answered.

"A *gringo*?"

"Yes, a tall one, with a pack on his back."

Jorge had been resting in a hammock strung between two of the posts supporting the corridor roof. He raised himself up, and then somewhat laboriously coaxed his feet into his boots that lay on the ground. With some unsure steps at first he proceeded towards the door. His wife eyed the situation from the entrance to the kitchen, wiping her hands on a well-used apron that hung from her thin frame. The two younger children took up positions where they could hear what was to be said, yet not be seen.

Jorge opened the door. Bill was ready to speak, but no words came at first. He studied rapidly the strong character revealed in the face dignified with such a large mustache.

"Jorge Valladares?"

"Yes, that is my name. In what can I be of service to you?" The arrival of a stranger at the door always prompted a cautious spirit. The presence of a *gringo* was a novelty, a most unexpected occurrence.

Bill continued to read the appearance of the man. Thick, graying eyebrows shaded dark eyes, which unlike others in his age group displayed amazingly white borders free of yellow tinges and blood veins.

"Well, *Señor* Valladares I know that you have never met me before, but I believe that you knew my father." The few neighbors at home were leaning out of their windows, or over a fence listening to the conversation.

"I knew your father?" He noticed that there was something dimly familiar in his looks.

The situation now began to amuse him, a *gringo* at his door, talking about him knowing his father. All of this was rather strange and a much unexpected event for the daily affairs of San Juan.

One of the neighbors who had been leaning against a fence suddenly slipped, catching himself, but not before the movement and accompanying noise attracted attention. Jorge decided to invite Bill to step into the house to continue the conversation.

Entering the house he felt an immediate change of temperature. Outside the sun was bleaching the houses covered with lime into a blinding white. Inside, the tile roof and adobe walls made it easier to accept the daylight hours. He caught in his nose the smell of damp earth and objects, some in the process of decay.

Jorge, in a mixed gesture of invitation and command, told his visitor to sit on a wooden stool located to one side of the room. The door was left open allowing the light to stream in like water. Particles of dust and pollen floated about, illuminated by the intense sun.

The three children vied for the opportunity to look through a hole in the cardboard wall that separated the one room adobe house into supposedly private areas.

They looked longingly and with amazement at his well made boots and the shine from his watch. It was a watch like the one that Doctor Bardales wore when he came to the health clinic in San Juan.

Jorge lowered himself onto his wooden chair and took up the conversation again.

"You're from the United States? A long way from home, aren't you?" Bill nodded in the affirmative. The comment seemed more like an incentive to speak than a genuine question.

Coming to the main point at hand he asked. "And your father, you said I knew him. Who was he?" Bill cleared his throat and asked if he might take the backpack off.

Jorge responded in a kindly way and excused himself for not having been more mannerly. Though not polished and of little secular education, he possessed common decency. His actions and words were guarded though. He had lived long enough to know that not all people were to be trusted. He knew well the proverb:

"Some have a fine face, but you can't see the heart."

"*Señor* Valladares, around 1970 you worked in the banana camps of the fruit company here in San Juan. I am right on that, aren't I?"

"Yes, I worked with the company between 1960 and 1985, twenty-five years." The question highlighted the curiosity of the moment.

"When you were with the company do you remember having worked with a Mr. Walker?" Jorge considered the question, laboring momentarily with Bill's pronunciation of Mister as well as the last name Walker.

"Walker?" He formed it into one more recognizable to Spanish pronunciation. The heavy eyebrows lifted, his face smoothed out losing its wrinkles.

"Mister Walker, yes I worked with him." The word mister soon became more anglicized. "He was a plant doctor. Yes, we worked here in the camps for two years. Jorge looked at his guest and now realized where he had seen the face before.

"Are you Mister Walker's son? Are you little Guillermito?"

"Yes, that's my name. My father used it as a nickname." Bill explained that Guillermito in Spanish was the same as Billy in English and the diminutive ending was an expression of endearment.

Jorge didn't seem to be much interested in the technicalities of language at this point; he was busy enjoying this unexpected occurrence in his life. An abundant smile came across his face, revealing the real nature of the man. He stood up and stretched out his hand shaking Bill's with vigor and deep appreciation. Bill's father had left many good memories with the men who worked with him in the camps.

"And your father Guillermito, or better now, Bill, because you are not a little boy. I can call you Bill can't I?" Though he struggled to correct the sounds his pronunciation of Bill was still done with a Spanish flavor to it, yet recognizable, and he would intersperse freely Bill and Guillermo in his conversation.

"Tell me, how is your father?"

The guest's somber expression reflected how the question was an emotional burden for him to hear.

"Well, *Don* Jorge." Bill used the Spanish term *Don* before Jorge's name to show him respect as an older man. "My father died about eight months ago."

The bushy eyebrows dropped and made the eyes supported by pleats of sun soaked skin even more indomitable in appearance. Jorge was mentally defying the reality of death, which was coming closer to his own door as well.

"Your father was a good man. He was fair, and he was kind. He helped us to help ourselves. He was not like some who saw us only as *campesinos*." The word *campesino,* or farmer used in this manner was understood as a pejorative. There was a pause before he added. "God never forgets good men."

The sudden arrival of the stranger had a decided effect on the world of the Valladares family. Reina, Jorge's wife, had left the kitchen at the back of the house and had ventured towards the front room where she could hear the conversation. When Jorge saw her he immediately called her closer. He explained who the visitor was, but the wrinkled brow and puzzled look said she didn't quite remember.

"Mister..." Then he said with more precision as he looked at Bill. "Or, Mister Walker. You know, the *gringo* who worked here with us in the camps." Seeing that she hadn't understood all of this he continued. "The fellow who helped us pay for the medicine when Ignacio was sick." The picture now came into focus.

"Oh, yes. Now I remember. Yes, him. This is his boy, well, how nice." She hurriedly wiped the remaining water from her hands, leaving her apron even more crumpled. She shook his hand with the same strength of character and genuineness as her husband.

Interrupting his wife Jorge found room to comment; "Do you drink coffee?" Without waiting for the answer he looked at his wife.

"Reina bring us some coffee please. You know, your father loved coffee, thick, black and sweet. They don't have coffee like ours in your country." A somber reflection darkened his face briefly. "He was a good man your father."

There was a pause, and then Bill spoke.

"Yes, I would be pleased to have a cup."

"Are you comfortable on that stool?" He rapidly obtained another dusting it with a work shirt that hung from a peg driven into the adobe wall. But, it was declined. "Did you come in the train today from Puerto Ángeles?"

"Yes I did. I stopped at a store down where they let us off and asked how to find you. A woman told me how to get here." One of the children showed his face from behind the cardboard and offered his observation.

"He spoke with *Doña* Inés." The boy had been trained to respect his elders, and therefore used 'Doña' a title of respect for an older woman. It was obvious that the stranger's arrival had spread quickly amongst the children. Bill looked over at the boy and smiled, prompting him to bashfully look at the ground.

Jorge was busy asking questions, barely allowing time to answer them when Reina came back with the coffee.

One of the cups had a small chip on the lip. The aromatic smell of the coffee brightened the conversation. True to tradition, it was thick, black and sweet. The cups were left with a yellow film inside, and the men's teeth also were tinged with the same stain after each sip.

Chapter 2
The Diary

Reina had returned to the kitchen where she was busy forming perfectly round *tortillas* with deft movements of her fingers. Five plantains were located close by, waiting to be sliced and placed in the frying oil. She shared her attention between the food that was cooking, and the firewood that she periodically inserted and withdrew to control the temperature of her simple but active clay stove. The preparation area was a waist high table. It was a thick slab of mahogany held up by four rustic legs also of the same wood. The simple meal being prepared enjoyed more attention from her than normal. True, it was the same as that which they ate every day, but there was a guest this time, that made the occasion special.

Jorge's children had sought out their friends to let them know who the visitor was, and to try and guess what he wanted in San Juan, or how much his boots must have cost.

They were identified as "Jorge's children", but in reality they were *hijos de crianza*. A term used for children given away by parents who didn't wish to have them, or couldn't afford to raise them. Older couples would take them in and raise the castaways, a hedge against future senility and the need for support. Jorge and Reina though had adopted the children with a desire to provide them with a home, as well as the love and the training that would weave the Valladares into a common fabric, a family.

In the area behind the house amongst some trees and numerous bushes, Jorge and Bill were carrying on an animated conversation. The young visitor listened respectfully as Jorge shared with him details of life in the banana camps, as well as the activity of his father with whom he had worked. Bill lent his ear not just out of cordiality. He needed the old man's help with the details of the diary if he was to find what he was seeking. Finding the diary was an unexpected turn-of-events in his life.

Shortly after his father's death, his mother had decided to move to an assisted living community where there would be no yard work, no upkeep. It seemed like a good idea. As the only child, he helped his mother with the work of packing, cleaning, and getting the house in shape for the realtors. He had been sitting at his father's desk, going through papers and mementos when he came across the diary. The covering was of black leather. It carried the characteristic smell of mold from the tropics. On its front cover were large embossed letters in gold, now dim and worn but still legible: DIARY OF DOUGLAS SCOTT WALKER-AGRONOMIST. He never knew that his father had kept a diary, finding it that morning was both a delight and a sad reminder of the loss of its author.

As he turned the pages and read the comments he could imagine his father speaking. It made his death even more unbearable. The burdensome cloud of emotion began to lift after a few moments. He even found reasons to laugh at times at what his father had said, or what he had done. With reverential respect he turned over the pages, thinking of how his mother was going to treasure this find amongst the papers. As he became absorbed in reading the words left by his father, one entry stood out. It read:

"Today, I was out to camp nine with Jorge Valladares. He is a simple fellow but excellent company. I wanted to check on the plantation, as there was a problem with Sigatoka in that area. The men recently sprayed the section and it looks like they did a good job of it. We rode up the river towards the base of the mountain, enjoying the monkeys screaming at us as we rode past. The company hasn't planted up into that area yet, so it is still virgin jungle, except for the recent gravel road that was put in for future growth. It looks like they need more gravel before the rainy season comes. At the head of the river we found a waterfall, not a big one, but nonetheless beautiful. I did a bit of fishing in the stream wishing all the time that Billy was with me. Jorge found something of interest. He had made a call on nature and came across what looked like an inscription on the rocks. A simple statement- *La Doncella*-, probably some property marker from an old land grant."

The passing comment about an inscription on the rock captured Bill's thoughts.

"*La Doncella*?"

"*La Doncella*?" He unconsciously translated the Spanish.

"The Maiden?" He had heard that before, but where?

He sat at the desk, pensive, allowing the expression to role about in his mind. Then, it came to him. He recalled where he had read about The Maiden.

His job as a field archaeologist with the state had taken him to Spain where he did research in the

National Library of the West Indies. He recalled a reference he came across to a Spanish ship, and the account of its Captain. He didn't remember all the details immediately. There was something though about the Captain being imprisoned for the loss of the ship, and how he eventually lost his mind. The ships name was *La Doncella*, or The Maiden. He sat there wrestling with the account trying to recall the details. Finally, his thoughts sharpened and brought him upright in the chair. His heart began to race.

"The Maiden! Now I remember."

The Captain languished in prison, and at the end of his days was considered to be mad. In his ravings he said the saints were punishing him for his sins. He needed someone to retrieve what he had hidden away and give it to the Church, hoping to buy the favor of God.

Bill looked carefully at the entry again. Could it be that his father and the worker had found the marker that the Captain had left?

"I can't believe this. It can't be just a coincidence. Did Dad find the marker? It has to be." He felt exhilaration, a rush of excitement as he recalled the full name of the ship and what he had stumbled upon.

"*La Doncella de Belén*; The Maiden of Bethlehem." He hurriedly searched the diary for more information. There was nothing. It was a lone entry of apparently not much importance to his father.

His father was an excellent agronomist, but he was not an historian, and not aware of much that had taken place in the colonial period of Latin America. Bill, on the other hand, was an avid reader of history. His job restoring colonial sites, and his training had made him familiar with the details of everyday life during that epoch.

Unknown to Bill when he found the diary, the way was being prepared for the lone entry to take him to the very spot where his father had seen the marker, and Jorge Valladares would help him find it.

A cool breeze coming in off of the sea swept the area behind Jorge's house. The old man and his visitor were still talking when Reina broke into the circle saying that she had prepared something to eat. They happily received the news, Jorge because he had a guest, Bill because he hadn't eaten since his supper the night before. The three bananas that he had purchased that morning before boarding the train had done little more than camouflage his hunger.

The two stood and Jorge took the lead towards the kitchen prompting Bill to follow.

The entire structure of the home, the front sleeping area and the kitchen was shaped like the letter L. The roof over the kitchen also formed a corridor as it extended out some seven feet on one side. This allowed the family to move from the room in front where they slept, to the kitchen in back, and all under cover of the roof, a design that was appreciated in rainy weather. The columns securing the corridor's roof were solid young tree trunks that had been cut precisely for their supportive role, one end of them being buried several feet into the earth. Besides shoring-up the roof they provided the hammocks with a place to be securely tied. The hammocks were a necessity for afternoon naps, or as a place to deposit oneself on sultry days.

The kitchen was a rather dark cubicle, but one from which necessary meals came. Inside a thick coat of lime on the *adobe* walls presented a clean white appearance, with exception of where it was rubbed off, or covered with soot and dirt. The smoke from the open fire built in the clay stove had blackened a portion of one of the walls. A dark, greasy looking mixture coated the limbs that served as rafters supporting the tile roof. The smoke rose with lazy, effortless indifference, seeking its escape through the openings between the tiles.

Bill's eyes adjusted from the sun outside to the shadowy interior of the kitchen. He noticed two plates on the table, with a portion of beans, rice, and some fried plantains on them. A cup of coffee for each plate sat to one side. Jorge invited him to take one of the empty stools that were tucked under the table. It was a basic meal, no frills. Its being offered in hospitality and sincerity, the best the family could provide, made it a meal to remember.

The floor was of packed earth, smooth and dark.

Two dogs were close by waiting for a stray morsel to fall, or to be tossed their way. There was a collection of fleas also that the visitor soon realized were enjoying a nice meal, at his expense.

The food rapidly disappeared with little conversation stopping the progress of chewing. When the two men finished, Bill stood and discreetly stomped his feet in hopes that some of the unwanted guests he had acquired in the kitchen might fall back on the floor. There they could take up lodging on someone else. Jorge suggested they go back outside and take up their conversation again. The idea was readily accepted.

Enjoying the shade and talking about life in San Juan, it came time for the conversation to take another direction.

"While I am here Jorge, as I have said, I would like to see some of the places my dad talked about. Dad had written a diary."

"A what?"

"A diary. It's like a book, you write down each day or whenever you want, what you saw or what you have done. Dad made mention of you in the diary. That is why I came to see you. You worked with him a good deal didn't you?"

"Oh yeah, we worked together almost all the time he was here." He looked down at the ground moving some dirt with one of the Sandals he wore. "It sure doesn't seem like that long ago."

"Jorge, do you think you could take me out to where camp nine was? I understand that there is a waterfall near there, and I would like to visit the area. My father spoke of it as something worth seeing. I would be pleased to pay you for going along, your time, whatever expense you would have." At the offer Jorge raised his head and looked with disbelief and amusement.

"No, you don't have to pay me. I can take you out to the falls. No problem, in fact, it is beautiful. The company never really developed that area. What little there was is all run down now." He hesitated in the conversation. "We will have to be careful, there are a lot of snakes up that way, *Barba Amarillas*. You have to watch out for them. When do you want to go? How about tomorrow? And by the way, where are you going to spend the night?"

Bill had seen a sign about a *hospedaje,* or inn when he had left the train, so he thought he could get a room there. When he made mention of his intention Jorge insisted that he stay with the family instead. They could provide him with a place to sleep, and would be glad to do so. These simple gestures of kindness, sharing what little they had, helped him understand why his father had appreciated people like Jorge and his family.

As they continued the conversation, one of the children interrupted, reminding his father that he was going to let him take the horse up to the family's plot of land. With patriarchal demeanor Jorge instructed him to do so, as well as how many *Camotes* he was to bring for supper. And, just as many fathers do he made mention of the obvious, reminding his son to take along something to dig them up with. Though gathering the machete and the hoe should have been a first step. But, when you are excited sometimes it's hard to think of all the details, like tools.

The conversation continued until Bill noticed his host was nodding his head periodically. His normal naptime had passed unobserved. So he stood up and asked Jorge's permission to wander around the area a little, in this way giving him some time to sleep.

It was the pleasant time of the afternoon when the cool sea breeze begins to be felt. Fires burnt in the earthen stoves of the local women, and the smoke flavored the air with a sensation of contentment.

As he walked slowly down the dirt road close to the house he saw a man leading his donkey in his direction. The poor animal was barely visible because of the load of firewood and *yuca* roots strapped to the beast's back. The load looked like it itself had sprouted legs and was walking. The owner like most men of the area wore the common attire. A shirt torn in several places, buttons missing and well soiled, and a pair of blue pants hopelessly large for his thin legs. The pants were saved from an embarrassing fall by a rope belt. Two rubber boots, not too large covered his feet. His face was gaunt, carpeted in selected areas such as his chin and upper lip with a beard a few days old. The crowning touch, a straw hat discolored by sweat, rain, dirt and the daily affair of his world. It was pushed back just enough to reveal his matted black hair. When sufficiently close Bill greeted him. The man smiled broadly revealing a mouth vacated by several teeth. Pointing to the load he said:

"Looks like you worked hard today." The man nodded his head to confirm the statement, and then silence followed. He offered another comment to the donkey's owner.

"You live here in San Juan?" Again there was an affirmative movement of the head. However, this time there followed a few words that were garbled, so much so that he didn't know what the man had said.

"My name is Bill Walker." Then he added. "Or, that is Guillermo. I am visiting with Jorge Valladares. You know him?" The man changed his machete from the right hand to his left in which he held the rope attached to the donkey's harness. There was a brief smile by both, and then the conversation that really never began ended. They parted company each moving on their way.

Bill continued exploring the area until the sun began to bury itself behind the mountains of San Juan. With no electricity the darkness of night came early. From where he was standing he could see the lights in the store belonging to Nicolás. The noise of a gas motor indicated that down there, near the store, there was a generator running.

He started back towards Jorge's house, enjoying the prelude to the night. The birds had stopped their animated conversations of the day. Some chickens would cluck, annoyed obviously as they vied for their roosting spots in the trees around the houses. The little *adobe* homes had no curtains, no glass in the windows. The family scenes within were subject to his consideration.

The flickering fires, somewhat more inviting than the insistent glare from electrical lights, cast shadows of strangely shaped humans on the walls. San Juan had not changed much since his father had lived there.

Instead of knocking at Jorge's front door, as he was now an official guest of the family, he went through a gated area on the side of the house. The gate was some wire fastened to a dry tree limb. A person pulled the limb up next to the post, dropping a leather thong over it leaving the wire pulled taut. It was a simple arrangement, yet it still took a few minutes for him to get it undone, get through and pull it back together again.

Jorge was there to greet him, along with his boy who had gone to the parcel of land with the task of bringing back the *Camotes*. They were standing next to the horse. It was frothy with sweat after the trek up the hill, and then back down with the load.

"Bill, come see what we will cook up for you tonight." He motioned for him to come closer, and then stretched out his hand with one of the *Camotes*, a golden brown sweet potato.

"How do you cook them?"

"Tonight we will roast them in the fire. You will like them. They are sweet, and they fill you up." That was a rather unadorned statement to the visitor's way of seeing things. But, for some in San Juan filling your stomach was more important than the taste of the food.

"Well, it is getting pretty dark and I think my wife has something ready for us now. Come on, let's go inside."

In the kitchen Reina was busy with the evening meal. Inside there was no gas stove, no refrigerator, no inside plumbing, nothing that would be viewed as a necessity by some women. She passed a good deal of her life doing what she was doing when the two men entered.

The little girl who had met Bill at the door in the morning was sitting next to one of her brothers on a wooden bench. They were busy with their hands, rubbing the grains of corn off of the dry ears. The corn fell onto a burlap bag that lay stretched on the floor in front of them. The reflected light from the fire in the clay stove would flicker, dancing on the faces of the children as they worked. Reina poured some coffee and handed the cups to her husband and the visitor.

"Well Guillermo, what do you think of San Juan?" He considered the question as he finished a sip of his coffee. Before he could answer Jorge continued.

"When your father was here he lived in one of the company houses. They are gone now. The company tore them down and took the materials to *Plan Grande* where they established the main plantation some years ago. Things have changed somewhat since then.

"Dad described a place, or a town where there was, oh, a little more movement. But, I think I like San Juan the way it is now." That statement was most welcomed by the family.

Jorge took another drink from his cup. Several drops of the black liquid hung suspended by the hair of his mustache. The dark beads shimmered like jewels in the light of the fire. The conversation was unhurried, inviting one to linger. The family was enjoying a precious moment of intimacy. Bill reflected on the contrast between the frantic pace of people in large cities, which fostered disinterest in others, and the bucolic simplicity of San Juan, where individuals lingered in the company of one another.

Reina interrupted the scene by handing him a plate. It was a simple meal, and his host was right. The *Camotes* do fill a person up.

The meal ended, and the conversation slowed. The time had come to make arrangements for sleeping. Each one then took his turn to visit the back yard, and thus avoiding being called upon to get up in the middle of the night to attend to necessary body functions.

One of the children would give up his bed for Bill's use. It was a frame of two inch by two inch Mahogany. Holes had been drilled at set distances up and down the frame, and a rope was passed back and forth through them. A piece of cardboard rested on top of the rope.

All shared the same sleeping area divided by what pretended to be a wall. It was constructed of cardboard attached to a wood frame about six feet high. This produced a feeling of privacy, to a degree, as it divided the room into where the parents slept and the area where the children would bed down. This separation of the room shielded from sight one area from the other. The sounds though were common knowledge by all who could hear, irrespective of which side you were on.

Bill pulled a flashlight from his pack and placed it on the floor next to his bed. Jorge set a wood pole against the door to secure it for the night. Then he inserted a steel bolt through a hole in the doorframe and into the jamb, a functional lock. There was a combination of grunting, squirming and a generous amount of scratching. When the candle was blown out the darkness became almost palpable.

Bill settled down for a good night's sleep. In the distance he could hear the low rumble of waves on the beach. The wind gently passed through the fronds of the coconut palms. Other trees responded in turn with their comments. With full stomachs, a promise of a new day ahead, the family and their guest were soon asleep.

Chapter 3
Reason For The Visit

His eyelids struggled to open as the morning light filtered through the spaces between the clay roof tiles. Slumbering bodies were summoned to another day's activity. In this half-awake state, Bill couldn't decide if he was comfortable or not. The warmth from the blanket was inviting, but the dampness from the earth floor a few inches below was hardly stopped by the rope and thin pieces of cardboard.

Rolling over several times trying to find the best spot didn't help either. He raised himself up, took stock of the situation, his body parts reporting in on their status. Clumsily he pulled on his trousers, socks, and then his shoes. Perching on the edge of the bed he stretched and yawned, trying to convince himself that another day had begun. The family had been awake for almost two hours. He had missed the best part of the day by their criteria.

He could hear muffled voices of men conversing as they passed the house. They were on their way to attend to their crops growing in the fertile soils of the mountain slopes to the west of the village.

He recognized another sound as well, one of the sounds from the night before. Somebody in the kitchen was grinding corn with a stone mortar. That was not all that was taking place in the kitchen. The sweet, pungent aroma of recently brewed coffee wafted through the air.

Reina was obviously busy in her domain, preparing the needs of the family in her unadorned kitchen. He couldn't hear Jorge's voice or that of the children. They had gone off to work on their plot of land.

Bill felt rested, but definitely somewhat scruffy and in need of a shower, as well as a change of clothes. The shirt was clammy, his pants also. The sweat had dried and left a residue of body oils. The door to the back of the house was open a few inches, allowing the light to slip through with no resistance.

Passing his hands over his hair he tried fruitlessly to press it down on the back of his head. It had stiffened into a rebellious position after having been laid on the better part of the night. When he was at last satisfied with the uselessness of the gesture, he stood and headed towards the door that led to the kitchen area.

"Good morning." Reina was pleased to see the guest, but she didn't voice any expressions of real meaning due to her burden of shyness.

"Oh, good morning. Did you pass the night well?"

"I don't know." A look of perplexed worry crossed Reina's face.

"You don't know?" What she had heard obviously startled her.

"No, I was too busy sleeping." Her face allowed a subdued smile at the humor of his comment. The words also indicated a measure of humanity in the foreigner, which served greatly to dispel her nervous apprehension at having a foreigner as a guest.

After inquiring about Jorge and the children, and other diplomatic and courteous affairs, he felt it best to find out where the family had their plumbing facilities located.

"Excuse me, but do you have a place where I can wash up." He knew already the location of the outhouse towards the back of the property. His trip to it the night before almost met with disaster. His flashlight narrowly missed falling into the dark abyss located the other side of the hole in the wood seat.

She gently pushed a stick of wood farther into the fire. Then, cautiously, yet with professional flair she removed a tortilla from the flat metal griddle resting over the flames. With the tortilla still in hand she took a step towards the door. She gestured towards the back of the property, and mentioned that there was a pipe that brought water down from the hill. He could wash up there.

He looked in the direction she was pointing and made out the area she referred to. Knowing that he would be in need of some items she pulled a red plastic bucket from a shelf. Inside the bucket there was a dry gourd bowl and a piece of soap. He politely accepted the implements and then proceeded to where she had indicated.

On his way he took time for a necessary stop to yawn and stretch out some wrinkles in his body. When about half way to the bathing area he recalled he hadn't brought his towel or the other items he needed. So, back he went to where he had left his backpack. Gathering up a towel, his razor, a mirror and other items, he again shuffled towards the back of the property.

The shower area was a collection of palm fronds tied in vertical positions to a wooden frame. This provided for a measure of covering, though at times a neighbor or family member would pass by and start up a conversation on some trivial matter while a person washed himself. Bathing in back of your house required some privacy, while bathing in the river was often done with little concern for any sartorial splendor. Slats of wood served as the flooring. They were placed in such a way as to allow the water to drain out between them.

The water coming out of the pipe was cool, but not shockingly so. He filled the bucket to the brim and placed it to one side, setting it on the slats of wood. Then he began the process of removing his clothes, hanging them on a nail and hoping that they wouldn't fall or be in the way. Lathering up his face he took hold of the mirror and began shaving. This task accomplished he turned to showering by dumping water on his head using the gourd and the bucket.

The bucket's capacity limited the amount of water used. He had taken this into account and used the water judiciously. After pouring the last gourd of rinse water over his head, then using his hands as a squeegee to remove the bulk of the water, he turned to drying himself with the small towel. The next step had him balancing on one leg struggling to put on his underwear, being careful to not drop them on the wet slats under his feet.

With this morning ritual performed, he gathered up his items and slipped back through a space between the palm fronds. As he walked back towards the house Jorge and the boys were coming in the side gate.

"*Don* Jorge, how are you this morning?"

"Hey, somebody finally got up. And look at that! He is all bathed too." Mornings were the best time of day for the old man.

One of the boys carried a small bucket with some fresh cow's milk. The inner surface of the pail was coated with a thick cream due to the liquids sloshing about on its trip down from the mountain. Jorge directed himself to one of the boys:

"Take the milk on into your mother." Then looking at Bill he asked.

"Have you had some coffee yet?"

"No, I just got up a little while ago.

"Come on then, let's see what my dear wife has for us this morning." Jorge and his family wished to make their guest feel welcome, like one of the family. They had little in a material way, and yet, common decency and human kindness was rooted in their personality.

He had been unknown to them until the day before, but, he carried the recommendation of the conduct of his father, and for this he was considered an honored guest. The father had developed trust and respect with men like Jorge. Now the son was using those credentials, and because of them being accepted as a friend.

The smell of freshly made corn *tortillas* was in the air, tempting hungry stomachs.

Reina had filled two plates with beans and then placed them on the table along with the *tortillas*, coffee and this morning a glass of warm milk with sugar, this was the menu. Normally the milk was used to make a soft cheese called *Cuajada*. Today though, some found its way to the table as a sign of appreciation for the visitor.

Holding a piece of a *tortilla* between his fingers Jorge soaked up the last of the juice from the beans on his plate. He then took up the theme of how they would get out to the falls at camp nine.

"What we can do is ask to borrow a *Burra de Línea* from Pedro Contreras. Ah, I should send one of the children to ask him now." He turned to his wife.

"Where is Santiago?" His little girl who was helping her mother answered.

"He is outside."

"Tell him I have an errand for him."

"Yes Papá."

Bill wasn't sure what a *Burra de Línea* was so he questioned his host about it. Hearing the inquiry by the young man provoked a smile from Jorge.

"I imagine you don't have *Burras* in the United States. Everybody must have a car, eh?"

"Well, no. Not everybody." Jorge reflected briefly on the comment before speaking.

"At one time the company had plantations up and down the coast. To get merchandise in and fruit out, the company established its own railroad system. They would bring in a train on the main line, and then on the spur tracks to the individual camps. We would load it up with bananas, and then it would return to Puerto Ángeles where the fruit was loaded onto cargo ships. From there the fruit went everywhere, Europe, North America, all over the world. When the company pulled out of this part of the country they left the rail lines. The government owns the train that runs from Puerto Ángeles to here. When you came into San Juan you were on the old main line, the spur lines no one uses but us. So, what we do is, we take a small flat cart of wood like this." He reached out and grabbed two knives from a jar on the table to illustrate what he was saying. Placing them side-by-side, and then drawing imaginary lines he continued.

"It is about five feet by seven feet, more or less. It has a flat area of wood like a table in the middle, you see, like this. We put old rail wheels on the cart, the kind like the trains use just smaller. Then we have two long poles, one on each side like these two knives. We take turns pushing it, or if you are by yourself, you have to do all the work." Anticipating what the young man would say, Jorge spoke up.

"They don't have a motor as you can see. It is pretty heavy and hard to get moving, but once it gets rolling along, it is hard to stop. So, that is one of the ways we get around, and that my young friend, is how we will get you out to camp nine."

Bill considered the explanation, picturing how he and Jorge would take turns pushing the heavy cart down the tracks. The uncertainty of what awaited them was made obvious by his look.

"Don't worry about it, we will take the boys along to help push. And now, eat your food. Hey, you don't have any *tortillas*." He turned to Reina.

"Do you have more *tortillas*?" Before she could answer Santiago stuck his head around the corner.

"Did you want me Papá?"

"Good, here you are. Run down to Pedro Contreras and ask him if we can borrow his *Burra de Línea*." The words had scarcely left his mouth when the boy ran off, excited with the assignment and the possibility of some coming adventure.

Jorge took a large gulp from his coffee, swishing it around in his mouth to wash his teeth of the residue of food that had stuck between them. His puffed cheeks revealed the flow of the liquid. He swallowed it, and then looked at the visitor.

"Guillermo, tell me, why do you want to go to the falls? Wouldn't you rather see where your father lived, or where the house used to be, that is the foundation because the buildings are gone now, or maybe the old company office? You know, your father spent a lot of time in those buildings. You can see where they were and imagine what it was like." Bill knew that the time would come when he would have to take his host into his confidence. His head turned slowly and he looked at Reina and her daughter standing by the fire. This pause in the conversation was unnatural, and the old man noticed it.

"Jorge, do you think we could go outside and sit?" Reina's dark eyes spoke with those of her husband, indicating a communication of feelings that comes with years of sharing life together. After a noticeable pause he replied with a serious tone.

"Of course we can." He stood up, straightening his legs which had stiffened a little, and then asked Reina if she could get some food ready for them to take on the trip. The two stepped outside and walked towards a Tamarind tree not far from the house.

"Jorge, I have something I want to consider with you that is of great importance to me. But, first I need to ask a favor of you." The old man displayed a puzzled smile.

"A favor? I don't know what we can do for you, but if there is something, well you can count on us to help where we can."

"What I am going to tell you I would like you to keep to yourself. You know what I mean, not Reina, or the kids, no one should know about the details of my visit." Jorge nodded his head in agreement though rather reluctantly.

"I told you that my dad had kept a diary. The little book about what he did each day. Well, in the diary he made mention that on a certain occasion you two were out by camp nine. According to the diary, while you were at the falls you came across some writing on a rock." At that point he stopped speaking, the absence of words marking a definite punctuation in the conversation.

"Do you remember where the spot was where you saw the writing? Think hard. It said, *La Doncella*."

The mustache moved about, Jorge's lips rising and falling due to the gestures of the face, a necessary act for deep thinking. The writing had obviously not made much of an impression on him, and it was many years ago. That brief minute of silence seemed unending to Bill. "Do you remember seeing it?"

"Well, we went out by camp nine on several occasions. And the matter of the waterfall, yes, there is one out there. But, writing on a rock?" He continued to wade through the fog of memories long past. "You know, I do remember something about that. But I don't remember what it said. What did you say was written on it?"

"*La Doncella*. But, that really isn't important now. What I want to know is can you take me to where you saw it?"

"Take you out there? That isn't hard. What might be difficult is finding this writing you want to see. It was a long time ago you know."

The words confirmed what Bill wanted to believe. His father and Jorge had found the marker. But, would he find what supposedly was left there? Would it still be there after all these years? The moment of doubt was unsettling. Bill knew that the time had come to bring Jorge into his confidence; it was now crucial to obtain all the help he could from his host. There was a need to weigh his words carefully, to choose exactly the right manner to present the situation to the old man. Slowly, articulating with great care and in a subdued voice, he began:

"I am going to tell you something. You may not believe it, or well; anyway, I want to tell you something. However, before I do, you must understand that it is best if no one finds out. If you and I can locate what is at the falls, it may be very important." The enigmatic and cryptic comments did little to help Jorge understand the seriousness of the moment.

"Let me start at the beginning. That marker that you found, the writing on the rocks, it was left behind by..."

"Papá, Papá, Pedro said you can use the *Burra*." Young Santiago had chosen a most inappropriate moment to interrupt the conversation with his sudden entrance.

"We are talking here Santiago can't you see!" Jorge noticed that his gruff reply had startled the boy, so he softened his words.

"We have something of importance that we are talking about, and you shouldn't have interrupted like that. Now, thanks for the errand and go help your mother ready the food. Tell your brother to get ready too. We are going on the *Burra* for a little trip today." The thought of a trip, something out of the ordinary, this more than compensated the boy for the harsh tone of his father.

"I am sorry, my boys are, you know, they are boys. Now, you were telling me about this writing that your father and I found. Why is it so important to you?"

The two continued talking for some time in the shade of the tree before they returned to the kitchen. When they did, Jorge prompted his wife to hurry with the food. He also requested that a small thermos of coffee, a thermos with a gaudy yellow flower motif on its side be prepared to accompany them on their trip.

Bill gathered a few items he thought might be useful and put them in his backpack. Soon enough the four left to find the *Burra* down by the line.

Reina stood in the kitchen doorway with her daughter and watched as the group left. The young girl's dark eyes focused intently on her Father and the boys. Then suddenly she turned to her mother and inquisitively asked:

"Are they going to the falls to fish?"

"I don't know my little one." She watched the troupe disappear down the road. Then she added.

"He is kind of a strange man, the young *gringo*, a curious sort."

Chapter 4
A Price To Pay

The two men spoke in an animated manner as they walked along. The boys, a few steps behind followed as best they could while being entertained by a stray dog who sought their company. Passing under some coconut palms they soon came closer to the rural store that belonged to Nicolás. Inés had seen the group coming down the road and was already drawing her conclusions on what they were doing. She was leaning out the window, her generous body filling the window space to capacity.

"Well, Jorge I see your friend found you." He adjusted his view in her direction. Cordiality prompted him to reply, though he would have rather ignored her.

"Yes, he found me. And how are you and Nicolás today?" His hesitation in answering was noticeable. That pleased her. She knew that everyone in San Juan had to speak with her, even if they didn't feel inclined to do so. After all, she was the wife of Nicolás.

"Fine. Nicolás should be back sometime today. He went to Puerto Ángeles yesterday afternoon with a load of Plantains in his new truck. Have you seen it, the new truck?" She relished mentioning the fact that it was a new truck, taking pains to draw out every syllable with precision.

"No I haven't. Maybe I will stop by later to see it. We must be on our way, so with your permission." He bowed his head slightly and began walking again.

Inés struggled to dissemble her perturbed feeling towards the old man. How abrupt his departure was. He didn't wait until she wanted to end the conversation. She called out before they were out of range of hearing.

"Where are you going in such a hurry? Old men like you shouldn't rush." Jorge knew it was better to not reply, as he might say what he really was thinking. He did manage a mannerly smile, though certainly not from the heart.

"Jorge, you and the lady don't seem to get along too well." That comment from his young guest brought him to a halt. He looked at Bill with a measure of incredulity at what had been said. Then after an appropriate pause, obviously reflecting on how to reply, his answer was expressed with caution.

"You don't know them Guillermo. Nicolás and Inés have been a source of grief for many in this area. He is not a man you can trust, and she is not a person to count amongst your friends." Realizing that his observation had unsettled the old man Bill felt it best to make amends.

"I am sorry Jorge if my words were out of place." The expression, given in this manner calmed his host. Then as if the matter were a joke he stated.

"If they are such a bad lot why doesn't somebody just take them out in a boat to fish and loose them somewhere out there?" Jorge looked out at the sea that had come into view from where they stood. He managed a restrained laugh that resembled more of a grunt.

"That's a thought, but.." He hesitated a moment. "God will see what needs to be done, when it will be done." It seemed that to say anymore would be unproductive, so, the two left the conversation there.

The boys had run ahead to Pedro's, the neighbor who was lending them the *Burra*. He was not the typical *campesino* or farmer, tall, thin, around 35 years old and from his appearance a man who was accustomed to hard work.

In the past he had been caught-up in the political struggles that plagued the country, using his life to support a movement promising better conditions. Those years had brought him close to death on several occasions. He finally realized that more was needed than changing a regime. People had to change inside, their qualities, ethics and morals. He saw no change in the leaders of the movement. He was fighting to replace one privileged group, with another privileged group. Wiser as to the reality of the world that surrounded him, he now focused on changing himself, while helping his children avoid the mistakes he had made. He was the type of neighbor you would wish to have.

When Jorge and Bill reached Pedro's, his children were sitting on the *Burra*. A shack made out of split bamboo served as the home for Pedro and his family. The rail line was just to the side of this house, some fifteen feet away. He was in front of his home sifting corn, which he accomplished by holding a bucket aloft and slowly pouring it out on a tarp. The lighter material, leaves and an assorted mixture of twigs would fall away blown by the breeze. This allowed the corn to fall and accumulate in a pile.

"Jorge, how are you today?"

"Fine, and you?"

"Well, I am in the middle of sifting this corn I have left. Santiago told me you need the *Burra*."

"Yes, if you weren't going to use it today?" Jorge had noticed two burlap bags sewed shut, apparently full of corn. Pedro was preparing part of his crop to sell what he had in the sacks.

"No, you know very well you are welcome to use it. I told your boy when he came that it would be here waiting for you. There is no problem at all."

"What about the corn, are you going sell it?"

"Yeah, I need to buy some school supplies for the kids." He raised a bucket full of corn into the air and then let it fall in a cascade onto the tarp. The wind caught the chaff and blew some of it back in his face, causing him to close his eyes for a moment.

"Books, pencils, you know how expensive it is to send the kids to school. I need to sell some corn to buy what they need." He stopped his work for a moment and looked at the pair. He then directed his attention to his children.

"I don't want them to go through what I have in life. I made too many mistakes. They need to learn something. Have a better future" There was a pause in the comments then he smiled and spoke up again.

"This must be the fellow that is visiting you. Santiago told me you had company."

"Yes, this is Guillermo Walker." Pedro lowered his bucket so he could step over and shake his hand.

"Are you working with the Peace Corps here *Don* Guillermo?" Surprisingly, his pronunciation of "Peace Corps" was without a Spanish accent. He had previous encounters with those who came to help with irrigation projects, schools, etc. and he had taken pains to imitate their intonation.

"No, I am just visiting with Jorge and his family." The old man spoke up.

"His father and I used to work together back in the company days."

"Oh, The Company. They had a lot of men up and down the coast at one time. Everybody had work then." He managed a grin reflecting on what he knew of the past. "Not much money, but a lot of work. Well, nice to meet you."

The presence of the visitors had attracted the attention of Pedro's family. Their curiosity had overcome their shyness and they ventured closer. Bill saw the wife and a generous collection of children that surrounded her. He wasn't enamored with the idea of everyone asking questions of him. Especially questions dealing with why he was going out to the falls. Shifting his attention to Jorge he mentioned that they had better get moving while it was early.

The *Burra* rested on the ground next to the house. The solid wood framing, steel wheels, a combination of parts and pieces cannibalized from a collection of machines and structures all spoke the same word, heavy. Bill studied the piece of equipment, which made possible this means of transportation.

On either side of the cart there were poles, stout and straight tree limbs around four inches in diameter. These were fastened to the cart and extended out from it on either end four feet. The poles could withstand the weight of a person, and that is what they had to do. One person at a time would push the cart, get it rolling at a reasonable rate, and then sit on one of the poles and allow the weight of the cart itself to keep up the momentum. Periodically, the one pushing would jump off and push some more to get the cart up to speed, and then, sit back down. The others might help out with a shove from their leg if they wanted to.

He felt a hand placed on his shoulder. Turning, he saw the smiling face of Jorge who was pleased with this opportunity to introduce his guest to the *Burra*. He began by giving some specific instructions on what to do if a person slipped while pushing the cart.

"You see the railroad ties on the line? While you are pushing sometimes your feet slip, or you get a foot caught on one of the ties, or you hit it with your boot and it makes your feet go out from underneath you. If that happens, you must let go of the *Burra*, and I mean immediately. If you don't, it will drag you along and take off more than you wish of the skin on your legs. You understand?" A congenial grin covered his face when the amused distrust of the foreigner was apparent.

"Oh, and one more thing I should make mention of, you have to watch out for the bridges. There are a few that don't have any ties because the floods carried them away. So, when we come to a bridge like that we call out, 'bridge!' Whoever is pushing can then jump back up on the cart. If you don't get back up, suddenly there is nothing underneath you and down you go into the water. The cart of course continues on." Bill had been listening in silence up to this point.

"No ties? What holds the rails in place?"

"The rails are thirty-nine feet long. They go from one side to the other, resting on the bank like this." He held his hands together illustrating what he meant.

"There is one on the river that we call 'the Bridge of Death'. Just one central post section is left in the middle of the river. The rails go out from either side, from the bank to the post. No ties anywhere, all of them were washed away. You won't have any problems as long as you push the cart fast enough to go all the way across. A couple of times they have fallen off. But, the water is deep in the river so you don't get hurt by the fall. That is, unless the cart hits you on the way down, or you can't swim. Can you swim?" A flush of anxiety swept across Bill's face.

"Don't worry my young friend. You will see it's easy. Well, almost easy." He turned to his children.

"Let's go boys!"

Between everyone pushing, lifting, grunting in unison, at times going in opposite ways it seemed, they were able to get the *Burra* up onto the rails. Jorge and Bill sat on the cart along with Santiago. Jaime, the younger of the two would be the first to push. The wheels began to turn and a low rumbling noise started, punctuated at intervals by the click at the joint of each rail.

The family waved the travelers on. The family dog couldn't resist the opportunity to bark, secure in the knowledge that they were leaving and wouldn't kick at him. The noise of the moving cart muffled Jaime's panting.

The *Burra* moved along past some houses, then the store. Bill saw where he had got off of the train on the main line. When he saw that spot he started thinking about what he had been told. He was sure that Jorge had said that the trains didn't use these rails anymore.

"Hey, Jorge! You did say that there aren't any trains on this line right? He moved a little closer to him.

"What did you say?"

"I asked about the trains. They don't use this line now. Isn't that what you told me?"

"You worry too much. You see those rails over there, the ones that go by the store. They are for the trains. This rail line is abandoned. It hasn't been used in years. There are times though when we meet another cart on the line. That isn't a problem, one of us just takes his cart off the tracks and lets the other pass." With a paternal reassurance he told him that before he knew it he would be at the falls.

They passed the last house in San Juan with the cart moving along at a steady rate. The scenery changed quickly. In the village there were signs of life, houses, smoke, children and animals running about, but now, dense jungle growth marked the end of man's encroachment.

The trees, bushes, plants and vines were always ready to assert their authority over the land if they weren't cut back or burnt. In some areas the *Burra* glided on the rails through a tunnel-like formation of vegetation.

At one point an abandoned grapefruit plantation appeared. The jungle reclaiming its domain had wrapped and intertwined itself with the grapefruit trees. The pink hue of the fruit stood out starkly from the dark green of the leaves and vines. Though the fruit was free for the taking, it fell and rotted in the dampness. Popular opinion was that grapefruit and lemons were to be used only for sick people, or for scrubbing household items like tables.

A curious troop of monkeys watched the passing cart. Their slender tails held them firmly in their arboreal homes. Creeks and lagoons with dark lily-covered waters hid what was beneath the surface. An alligator showed little more than its eyes. When Bill saw it, he started thinking about the bridges. Jorge had said that at times the carts fall from the rails. Thinking about the possibilities, he felt it was best to stop analyzing what might happen.

Jaime was sitting on one of the poles that extended out on either side. Since the cart was moving along nicely, a gentle slope making for little resistance, he could sit and push occasionally with one leg. They had about five miles to travel from San Juan to where the old camp was located. Bill soon realized that this mode of transportation wasn't as unnerving as he had imagined. Though on one of the shorter bridges that crossed a creek, he did start thinking about which way he should jump in case it became necessary.

The bridge crossed a body of water that was more like a lagoon than a stream. The rails were noticeably bowed to the left. When the last big hurricane hit the coast, the rushing water would pick up trees, logs or anything else it its path. The flow, as it rampaged towards the sea, would continue to grow as it descended from upstream, gathering strength and size from hundreds of streams that added to its volume. Bridges that were in the path would be stripped of their ties, or undermined and brought down. At times the flow would back up behind interlocking logs that had formed a dam. Finally, the force of the water behind the logjam would be great enough that it would bend the rails and then burst forth in chaos.

It was difficult to imagine such storms on a day like this one with the sun filtering through the overhead growth, the sweet, pungent smell of flowers in the air. The serenity belied the reality of tropical storms and their fury. It was a lazy moment. There was much to see, all new, all exciting. It was an experience to remember.

Jaime changed with Santiago and the cart had a fresh source of energy. Characteristic of youth, the boy was using more strength than good sense. He wildly pushed the *Burra* making it speed along the line. Soon enough this initial release of energy dissipated, and he settled into a more balanced and sustained approach to his task. He would push the cart for a distance, and then, he would sit on one of the poles, going back to pushing when it slowed down. It wasn't long before the *Burra* was allowed to lose momentum. It slowed, Santiago pushing only occasionally with one foot. Then it stopped.

"Well, here we are." Jorge made the announcement and then began to coax his body off of the cart. After sitting too long in one uncomfortable position his bones had begun to remind him of his age. A good stretch helped and then he looked about him. There wasn't much to see outside of jungle and the remains of some old foundations. Jaime stood up on the *Burra* examining the area. His brother was pleased to lie on the cart and rest himself.

Nothing of the camp remained. In fact, if you hadn't seen it, as Jorge had, then it was difficult to imagine what the remnants of the foundations were. The company had dismantled the buildings to use the materials in another camp. What the company hadn't taken, the people of San Juan or the jungle had.

Bill took hold of the nylon sack he had brought with a few items inside. He slung it over his shoulder and then walked over to where Jorge was standing.

"At one time we had about a hundred people here, more or less. Now there are two families who live in this area. The rest have gone on to take up life elsewhere. It has changed since your father was here." For a moment, he felt the frustration, the inevitability of old age.

"So, how do we get to the falls?" The question brought Jorge back to the present.

"Over there. We take a trail to the river, and then go upstream. I imagine that the old road isn't much more than a pathway, but we can take it all the way up." He called the boys to help and amongst all of them they moved the *Burra* off of the line.

"There, now if someone comes down the line we won't be in their way." He let out a sigh of relief, the breath moving the hairs of his mustache. One of the boys grabbed the net bag that contained the food and then followed the rest as they started for the river.

A few steps from where the trail began Jorge stopped and took out his machete.

"We have to watch for snakes, especially farther up the trail. A *Tamagás* or a *Barba Amarilla* can kill a man, and they are fast."

Bill looked at the machete, wishing that he had one as well. However, he did see a stout stick on the ground. Bending over he grabbed it. With his hands gripping the stick firmly he made a few imaginary blows on the ground.

"This thing may not be a machete, but it will sure change a snake's outlook on life." Upon hearing that comment, Jorge shared his own.

"I have seen snakes so big, that why; they could bite a stick like that in two."

The boys accepted that as solemn truth. Bill felt the story had grown through the years as much as the snake had.

Here they were, four people overshadowed by the immensity of the jungle, walking, and occasionally tripping down a trail headed for what lay ahead, though what lay ahead was an unknown at this point. The two boys imagined endless adventures.

Bill would just start to enjoy the beauty of it all when he would remember Jorge's warning about snakes. His eyes would immediately shift to the ground.

No breeze was felt, though high up the limbs and leaves were moving, as some gentle wind would stroke the tender parts of trees. The moist heat made the sweat run down his back, soaking his shirt, which clung to him like an extra layer of skin. The sound of running water became louder until they came to its source, the river.

It wasn't an exceptionally large stream, just some 30 feet wide. The waters swept past at a healthy pace, creating a gentle breeze which coaxed the vegetation, growing right up to the river's edge, into a rhythmic swaying. The river played the role of arbitrator between two opposing segments of jungle. Both sides pushed towards each other, but were unable to cross the water. Bill breathed deeply and wiped the sweat from his brow. He turned his head to hear what Jorge was saying.

"Just a short distance up the river is the place we are looking for. Don't expect too much from the falls, it isn't that big you know. Most of the water in the river comes from smaller streams that join in farther up from here."

"Jorge, do people come up here?"

"No, not much now. There aren't any crops up this way. A few banana plants or papayas, that is all. So once every so often you might have someone come up looking for food. Maybe a hunter, someone fishing, it is all government land now. When the company pulled out all the land went back to the government. The company never owned it, they just leased it." He paused, lifted his hand to his hat adjusting it.

"Well, are you ready to keep going?"

"Yeah, fine, let's go. With a serious tenor to his voice the visitor asked his host.

"Do you think you will be able to recall where you saw it?" The question didn't escape the attention of the boys. The reason for this sudden trip to the falls was unknown, but the trip not unwelcome.

"I think so. Maybe it will take some time because the area has changed. Quite a few years have gone by since I was here with your father. The storms have come and gone, plants have grown up. But, we will find it." Discerning the apprehension on Bill's face, he added.

"We will find it, stones can't move by themselves." With that, he turned and once more took the lead.

Occasionally Jorge would swing his machete to cut a vine or a plant. But, for the most part they were able to trample down or move aside what lay in their path. The old road, though now only a narrow trail, still provided a path they could follow. The crushed stone that had been laid down didn't allow the plants to grow as freely as they wished to.

The sudden, jarring squawk of a parrot sitting in a tree captured Bill's attention. It wore with much pride beautiful green feathers in an arrangement that contrasted sharply with the small tufts of red and yellow plumage on its wings and head.

After walking some forty minutes Jorge stopped.

"Listen! Do you hear that?" Through the jungle he could catch the sound of falling water. "We are close now. We have just a little more walking."

Hearing the sound renewed everyone's energy. As they approached the falls the sound grew louder and louder until they came to where the trail veered to the right. Jorge followed the path. Heavy strokes from his machete fell on the plants and vines, which had asserted their authority. They emerged at the bank of a flowing stream. An abundance of rocks on the bank indicated that in the rainy season volumes of water came cascading down the watercourse. Upstream, some 150 feet, threading its way through plants and vines clinging tenaciously to the rocks was the waterfall.

"Do you see that flat spot there?" He looked keenly, showing great interest in the question.

"Yes, I do."

"That is the spot where your father and I would leave the mules. Now, the day when I found the writing he was looking in the pool at the base of the falls and I went, let's see, over there as I recall. That's it! Over there, by where the little cliff is formed near the falls. Come on!

The sound of moving rocks on the riverbank hitting one another echoed about as their feet displaced them. A mist from the falls, though slight, could be felt in the air. The humidity and heat created a lush green house environment near the water.

"O.K. Let me think a little now. I believe I went this way and your father was over there." They moved closer to the area that Jorge had pointed out.

"Now, my young friend you have arrived." Those words seemed too long in coming. Now, finally, he was in the spot.

"How do we find it?" His question was sudden and to the point. Jorge thought a moment while he pushed on his back, coercing a few bones back to where they should be.

"We dismounted the mules, I came this way." As he relived the events of that day, as best he could, his eyes came to rest upon the boys who were intently watching him.

"Why don't you two go look around the river? But, be careful and watch for snakes. No fooling around either." The boys shuffled their feet reluctantly as they wanted to know what this was all about. A serious look from their father sent them away at a faster pace. He waited until they were not so close and then returned his thoughts to the matter at hand.

"So, your father was there, and I was here." He began to walk trying his best to mimic his actions as he recalled them.

The vegetation was thick at the base of the rock cliff that rose above them 50 feet. Jorge swung his machete from the right to the left. Behind him, Bill was gripping his walking stick firmly. He watched amongst the plants for any sign of movement, for any writing. SWOOSH! SWOOSH! The machete laid aside the plants. Jorge straightened himself and then began to mutter something trying to bring his memory into focus.

"Where was the spot? I know it was right here close by." Jorge continued the conversation with himself, but, his companion was more attentive to the brush and what might be moving in it. The machete continued laying aside the vegetation, the broad leaves of a Malanga plant falling before the steel of the blade. Then, he thought, yes, that he saw something.

"Here it is! The writing, just like I told you." Bill looked over his shoulder and saw the outlines of some letters crudely cut into the rock.

"Here, let me clear some more plants for you to see better." SWOOSH! SWOOSH! "Now, you can see them clearly, can't you?" Though carved with little precision, they spelled out, ' *La Doncella*'.

He moved closer to the inscription so that his fingers could feel for themselves the letters. Moss covered the depth of the cuts in the rock, masking the marker left so many years before. He mentally reviewed the account of the diary that he had read many times since its discovery. And now, here he was, here it was.

"I want to show you something Jorge." Quickly he walked over to where he had left his nylon bag. He opened it and pulled out a well-used copy of a book, a book of life in the New World and of the Spanish colonies. Dropping the bag on the ground he excitedly went back to show him. Thumbing the pages as he walked he endeavored not to trip because of the distraction.

"Here, look at this! This is a brief account of Captain Amadeo Rodrigo de Sevilla." Jorge's expression reminded him that all the details had not yet been explained.

"This is the Captain that left what we are looking for."

"Ah, this is the one who was the master of *La Doncella*." Now the two stood on common ground in the conversation.

As Bill explained needed details, the boys were busy throwing rocks into the river. Santiago jumped from one sand bar to another, peering into the waters. His younger brother, Jaime, was close behind. It required little to entertain them; time to relax was a joy in itself. They, like most children of the area, spent little time in enjoying the energy of youth. The hardships and responsibilities of life were thrust upon them early.

Jaime jumped ahead of his brother this time, his two feet landing solidly on the gravel. As he passed a tree rooted in the stream bank he felt a sharp pain from a thorn jab in the calf of his right leg. His pants were rolled-up, so he looked down to remove whatever it was that stuck in his leg. What he saw were two tiny slits or dots in his skin that oozed with a small amount of blood and venom mixed together. Raising his eyes he saw the thick body of a coiled viper near the roots of the tree stump. It wasn't a thorn that had stuck him. He had been bit, and working its way through his body was the venom of a *Barba Amarilla*.

He raised his voice out of terror more so than pain. All the stories he had heard of men who had been bitten rushed through his head in rapid succession. Men who had chosen to cut off their arm, or leg with a machete rather than die from the venom.

"Santiago, Santiago, a snake has bitten me." Hearing his brother's words brought a chill over him. He looked for a stout stick, finding one he gathered it up and ran to where his brother stood.

"Where is it?" Jaime raised his hand, shaking and pointing to the riverbank where the snake still lay coiled and ready to strike out again. Santiago began to beat the snake violently as it repeatedly struck at the stick seeking to escape. Soon it lay limp and disfigured from the blows.

Jorge and Bill had heard the boy's yelling and had gone to see what was happening. When they found them Jaime was sitting on the ground with his leg outstretched.

"Papá, a snake has bitten Jaime."

"A snake!" The old man stumbled down the bank, ignoring the years his body carried. Bill came behind him. "Where is it?"

"I killed it. There it is by the big root coming out of the bank." Jorge squinted and fixed his eyes on it.

"It's a *Barba Amarilla*. Miserable animal." Turning to his son, who was dazed and in shock due to the thought of what had just taken place and the venom's destructive process, he asked.

"Where did it bite you?"

"Right here." The words were spoken between sobs.

Shortly after a *Barba Amarilla* bites the pain begins, like a hot iron on your skin. The shock takes a heavy toll as well. Jorge took control of his paternal emotions and displayed the qualities of a man of experience. He knew he had to get to a source of the anti-venom.

He considered what needed to be done. They must make a fast trip back to the *Burra*, and then on to San Juan. It was the only option. Bill agreed and volunteered to carry the boy to the cart. Santiago and his father helped lift him up onto Bill's back. Feeling the weight of the boy he remembered his tote sack and sent Santiago to get it. Jorge took the lead as they hurriedly sought out the trail back to the *Burra*.

The return trip was made in record time. Little thought was given to the heat or the pace. However, Bill couldn't ignore the branches and vines striking his face and eyes as he ran down the trail.

Upon reaching the rail line they laid the boy on the ground. Then the three struggled to place the cart back on the rails. Santiago would begin pushing.

Bill would replace him when he got back his breath.

The boy's vision had begun to blur, his breathing was labored, and his head pounding. The snake's venom was wreaking its havoc.

Jorge tried to position him on the cart, providing as much comfort as possible. He looked upon the round face while he recalled memories of similar scenes and men he had known. Men with disfigured limbs, necrotic flesh, dead.

The bite of a *Barba Amarilla* was to be feared.

Chapter 5
No Time To Loose

I t was debatable how long Santiago could keep up the pace, pushing the *Burra* with such an unbridled desire to reach home. His brother's eyes were closed. The listless body of the boy was making scarcely any movement, except that which was mandated by the moving of the cart as it jumped, jerked and swayed with the contour of the rails. The rolled-up pant leg revealed that the leg had begun to swell. Jorge said that they could expect him to start bleeding from the mouth or his nose, or if a large amount of venom had been injected, from his eyes or ears. So far there wasn't any massive hemorrhaging, which was a good sign.

"Bridge!" The sudden yell from Jorge took Bill by surprise. Santiago jumped up on one of the poles, lifting his legs. The cart crossed over the water, momentarily suspended above it only by the two steel rails. At the speed they were traveling the bow in the rails was more noticeable, causing the cart to shift rapidly to the right and then back again.

Bill began to think about the inscription. He was so close. What if someone saw where the plants had been chopped back, or worse, the writing? He reassured himself by recalling Jorge's words that very few people ever visited the falls. After all, who would understand the meaning even if they did see the inscription? His father and Jorge hadn't. Maybe what had been left in the cave wasn't there anyway. With these thoughts tormenting him, he worked himself into a state of panic. That is until a feeling of guilt descended upon him. He was only thinking of himself. Little Jaime could die, and he was thinking only of himself. He cleared his head and looked at Santiago who was still pushing the cart at a furious pace.

Jorge was lamenting the entire episode as he monitored his boy. To be bit by a *Barba Amarilla* was nothing of little consequence. He had been bit twice himself. There was the time when he was cleaning the patch of land where he planted the coffee. Yes, he had been bitten, but he survived. Many have made it to the clinic in time. Though, some hadn't. He labored with his thoughts. With determination he convinced himself that they would get Jaime to the anti-venom in time. They just had to.

Death wasn't uncommon in San Juan, but it was accepted with the same feeling of helplessness as anywhere else. The emotional anguish of those left behind was never fully eliminated, irrespective of how many times a neighbor, in a clumsy gesture of supposed comfort added some unfeeling comment.

The return trip seemed an eternity when in reality it had been made in record time. The cart rolled into San Juan with Bill pushing. Santiago had finally given up and needed to be relieved. Bill was now at the end of his strength as well; his legs were shaking from the strain. The constant panting had dried the saliva in his mouth and throat into an impenetrable coating. Jorge looked about the area, and then back at his son.

"You are going to be all right son, just a little while longer." He placed his hand on his son's head. There was little response or recognition of the gesture.

Casimiro and Gregorio, two of the older neighbors in the village, were sitting on a plank bench in front of a nearby house. They stared at the passing cart as it slowed to a stop. Their vision wasn't what they had enjoyed as young men. Yet, they still saw sufficient to remind them of what they had seen on many occasions in the past.

When the fruit company still operated in the area it wasn't uncommon to see men brought in from the camps. Some on carts, just like Jaime, others slumped over a saddled horse or mule. Family or friends would bring them in to the company's infirmary. The men had been hurt on the job, while others had malaria or hepatitis. There were those who had been hacked with a machete. The latter were more prevalent on paydays when revelry was sought as a means to forget the reality of life in the camps.

The cart had slowed sufficiently so that Santiago and Bill could use their legs as a brake. When the cart was fully stopped Jorge sent his oldest son to inform his mother of what had taken place. The running boy, sweaty and disheveled would be sure to attract the attention of the neighbors. Word would spread rapidly.

Jorge had been considering what to do during the return trip. He had decided that instead of taking the boy to the local health clinic it would be better to get him to the hospital in Puerto Ángeles. The health clinic in San Juan, like those in other villages couldn't provide the care that the boy might need.

A sympathetic woman named Margarita supervised the local clinic. Her main function regrettably was to instruct everyone to go to the hospital in Puerto Ángeles as the Ministry of Public Health hadn't sent any supplies to San Juan for some time. This shortage of medicine was due to the lack of international credit. Medicine couldn't be imported from the foreign pharmaceutical companies without payment being made first. No money, no medicine. No medicine, people died. It was a simple equation. Money was the important factor, not life or mitigating suffering.

Casimiro and Gregorio began to walk over to the cart where a woman and her children were already standing. Jorge was on his way to arrange some transport for the boy. He passed the two men on his way.

"Jorge, what's happening?"

"A *Barba* bit one of my boys."

"A *Barba*! Miserable animal. When did it happen?"

"This morning out at camp nine. With your permission, I have to talk to Nicolás about taking us to the hospital."

The two men readily excused him to tend to matters. Normally a casual meeting of the patriarchs of San Juan would last a half hour or so. Today though, there was no time to lose.

As he neared the store he saw the new truck parked nearby. Some boys were busy washing it, struggling with the mud as well as the abundant bug remains on the front that had accumulated from the last outing.

He climbed the steps rapidly, his feet landing heavily on the wooden stairs announcing his arrival to Inés. She was looking over the newspaper brought from town. Jorge's abrupt greeting wasn't to her liking. Barely lifting her head, she managed to recognize his entry.

"Oh, Jorge, back already I see." She continued looking over the paper.

"*Doña* Inés, could I speak with *Don* Nicolás please?"

His having passed by formality with his words indicated that something was not as it should be. Though she understood perfectly well what he had said, it was not in her nature to be prodded into action.

"What was it you wanted?" She mumbled with her head bent over the reading material. The words almost slurred as they left the plump round mouth with its thick lips.

"I said I want to speak with your husband." She turned her head towards him, staring, giving the impression that she was trying to decipher his petition. Finally, she lifted her burdensome arms from the counter, heaved a rather laborious sigh, and disappeared behind the curtain that served as a door.

He turned from the counter and began to go back and forth, nervously, hitting his hands together. Outside, a beautiful blue sky covered San Juan. The waves were rolling up on the beach with kindness today, a gentle breeze pushing its way through the palm fronds. None of this appealed to him, his mind being focused on one thing, his boy.

He wanted to blame himself, though he knew that made no sense. Some persons, like Nolasco his neighbor, had been bitten while in their own house. He was a strong, young merchant marine home visiting his wife and family. As he entered his front door he wasn't aware of the snake coiled to one side of the entry seeking the shade. It was just being in the wrong place at the wrong time, that's all. The poor fellow died, he died. This recollection tortured Jorge's emotions.

"Jaime is young, we will get him to Puerto Ángeles. He is going to be fine." As he moved about he continued to mutter to himself.

The curtain abruptly was pushed to one side. A man of 55 years of age with a checkered shirt entered. It was opened sufficiently to show the hair on his chest and a large gold chain supporting a medallion of a saint. Nicolás wiped his mustache of the white cheese that he had been eating.

"Jorge, what's new old man? Inés said you wanted to see me." He could be so charming when he chose to do so.

"Yes, Nicolás, I need your help." He walked closer to the counter. "My little boy, little Jaime, he has been bitten by a *Barba* and I must get him to Puerto Ángeles."

"A *Barba*! That's bad, real bad. When did it happen?"

"Around noon. We were out at camp nine, and the two boys were down by the river and he didn't see the snake. You know how that is. What I need is to take him to the hospital in Puerto Ángeles. That is why I am here. Can you take us in your truck? It is the fastest way, you know that."

"Is he throwing up or bleeding yet?"

"No, but his leg is swelling. What do you say, can you take us?" The request was considered.

During this conversation, Inés had been behind the curtain listening so as not to miss any of the details. Unaware that she was only two feet away Nicolás shouted for her. This sudden occurrence sent her surprised heart into an erratic beat. Gathering her composure she moved the curtain to one side. Not too quickly, never too quickly.

"Yes, what do you want?" She knew very well what was taking place.

"Tell Francisco to get a hammock from out back and string it up in the truck." That was a good sign.

"Then you will take us?"

"Sure, what else can I do? Where do you have him?"

"He is over by the rail line to the old camps. I appreciate this, I will pay you for the trouble." Nicolás would have no trouble in finding a way to be repaid. He was not one to serve others out of largesse, or kindness.

Inés didn't like the way her husband was being so cooperative. She began to suspect the worst about his sudden desire to help out Jorge. She reviewed the details, knowing that something was amiss. Her face revealed her thoughts.

"He is looking for a way to get back to Puerto Ángeles, which is what he really wants. And, what will he do when he gets there?" She knew her husband well. She could imagine how he passed his time in town, and in the company of whom he would employ it.

Jorge headed back to the cart where several neighbors were already gathered. Bad news traveled fast in San Juan, any news really, but in particular reports of the sufferings of others. Santiago had gone to the house to tell his mother what had taken place. He found her washing clothes on a scrub board out back of the family home. When he informed her of the nature of his sudden arrival she immediately dropped everything and headed for the cart. Her hurried pace and distraught countenance informed those that saw her that something dire had taken place. Not willing to be the last to know the particulars, the neighbors took up following.

When she reached the cart she sat down next to her son, her legs draped over one side. Oblivious to the gawkers and the crowd she began running her fingers through Jaime's hair. Though he wasn't her biological child the pain was just as wrenching as if he were. The shared memories and hopes were just as trampled on, the helplessness just as poignant.

Bill was turning somewhat pale, not just from the exertion of the return trip, rather from the remorse he felt seeing that this entire matter was of his making. If they had not gone to the falls none of this would have happened. What a turn of events when he was so close. He was right there, just steps from it most likely. Hopefully, no one was going to ask too many questions, be too inquisitive, or prod for information as to what he was doing out at camp nine. The feeling of guilt began to give way to worry. He couldn't help but think about the boy. But, he was so close. He was sure about Jorge, as he would say nothing. Nothing intentional that is. Yet, there might be the slip of the tongue, or the wrong thing said to the wrong person. His mouth was getting drier, his heart punctuating the anxiety with well-defined beats.

Nicolás had backed his truck up to the front of his store. Raúl his oldest boy, along with a couple of the hired men hurried to get the hammock into place.

The truck was a Japanese model, a Hino. A wooden cargo box measuring eight feet by fifteen feet had been built onto the frame. Raised above this box was a rail that ran the length of the truck bed. On this rail a tarp could be suspended, with half of it slanting either way forming a roof. Today though, Jaime was going to be the load, so there was no need for the tarp. The hammock instead would be tied to the rail so it could swing free in the back of the truck. It was the best way to transport a sick person over the poorly built and neglectfully maintained gravel roads.

With the group gathering at the *Burra*, the movement at the store, the dogs in an apoplectic frenzy, there was no one in San Juan that wasn't aware of something out of the ordinary taking place.

"Raúl, are you done tying the hammock yet?" The perturbed note of the words landed heavily upon him.

"Yes, just about. There, now it is done." He gave a tug on both ends of the rope, and then looked at his father. With hopeful hesitancy and a note of fear in his voice, he ventured to ask his father a favor. "You want me to go with you?"

"No, you stay here." He didn't want his boy under foot in Puerto Ángeles. He would only be in the way. The possible report to his mother about his father's conduct in town wouldn't be desirable either.

The son, though a man himself physically, was emotionally truncated and indecisive to an extreme. Nicolás never made any effort to develop a close relationship with him, and the mother was blamed for the breach. The father saw his boy as being too much under the tutelage of his mother, from whom the boy didn't withhold any secrets. Especially any report dealing with his father's activity when not hemmed in by the wife's surveillance

Inés was standing at a distance with her hands on her hips. A perturbed look was on her face. Nicolás moved decisively toward the cabin of his truck, scattering some boys and a dog or two that were in his way. He grabbed the steering wheel and swung himself up onto the seat, started the motor, and began his maneuvering towards the *Burra*. Jorge tried to clear a path for the truck to back up.

"Careful! Here comes the truck! Back away there! Will you boys please get out of the way!" The motor switched from high-pitched tones to low grumbles as it rolled across dried mud holes left from the last rains. It stopped, a loud hiss of air indicated the brakes had been applied.

"How do you want to lift him?" Bill's question prompted Nicolás to turn his head fixing his attention on him. His expression changed somewhat as he gave consideration to the visitor, thinking to himself;

"So, this is the gringo they told me about. He sure looks a mess. I wonder what he is doing here."

"I'll jump up in the truck." Jorge acknowledged Bill's suggestion. He then cradled Jaime in his arms and tried to lift him. His body wouldn't cooperate, not after what he had been through.

"Just a minute!" Nicolás' authoritative command had brought a halt to everything.

"Patricio, Rafael, help him lift the boy up into the truck." The two men immediately came to his aid. Seeing that Nicolás had assumed command, another neighbor joined Bill to help place the boy in the hammock. Jaime groaned with pain, breaking his mother's composure. A neighbor of about the same age moved next to her for support.

"Courage Reina, they will get him to the hospital."

"Be careful, let him down slowly! Easy, easy." Finally, the boy lay in the hammock. Beads of sweat clung to his face while others formed a path rolling over his cheekbone. The swelling and discoloration of the leg was obvious to all.

"Reina, I'll let you know as soon as I can." After many years of marriage they could communicate much in few words, and Jorge's eyes told Reina a great deal. The anxious mother could do little more than shake her head in acknowledgement of her husband's statement.

"Santiago! Go back to the house with your mother. You will have to take care of everything while I am gone."

There was a brief discussion as to who would ride in the back with Jaime, and it was decided that his father and Bill would do so. One of the local men who worked for Nicolás rode up front with his boss. The engine came to life. Nicolás hit the accelerator several times with his foot, racing the engine. The people parted to let the truck pass. Then with a sudden lurch, which sent the hammock swaying, they started off on the trip to Puerto Ángeles and the hospital.

Chapter 6
The Hospital

Bill and Jorge held onto the sides of the truck doing what they could to not fall, and at the same time keeping an eye on the boy suspended in the hammock. Jaime would swing and roll with the gyrations of the vehicle. The concerned father was grateful that the hammock and its ropes absorbed the worst of the jolts.

The trip to Puerto Ángeles in the back of a swaying truck was not an incentive to travel. The road had been surfaced with gravel originally, now chuckholes sprouted up in colonies testing the skill of the driver. Nicolás was schooled in the intricacies of driving over such terrain. The truck would swerve from one side of the road to the other, trying to avoid the larger and deeper holes, which was not always possible.

The road followed more or less the same course the train tracks did. In some spots the two would share the same bridges, which were constructed of wood beams splitting with age. As vehicles, and especially the train, crossed the wooden structures they would coax loud cracking sounds from the support beams, indicating that they would soon make their last gasps before crashing into the rivers they straddled.

The truck passed by a man and a woman waiting at the side of the road with their newly made clay pots. These were partially wrapped in banana plant leaves for protection and gathered securely inside a fishing net arrangement of vines. Bill concluded that the couple must be on their way into town where they could sell the product as kitchen vessels.

Most from this area would travel by bus into town. Though such a trip was infrequent, and undertaken only if they had the money. They would travel on foot from their houses back in the bush and appear at the edge of the road where they would wait. Sometimes the wait seemed interminable. The bus could pass by at almost any hour, as its arrival depended on the driver having sobered up sufficiently to drive. They were old school buses imported from abroad that had been refitted with diesel engines, and then used for public transport.

In the excitement to get Jaime into the truck, Bill had left his tote-sack behind with Santiago. So, now he didn't have his passport or any identification with him. His money, most of it in traveler's checks, was at Jorge's house. He had no papers, nothing of money, extremely dirty with no idea of where this whole matter would end. The situation was not looking good.

"Hey, Jorge!" The worried father heard Bill call out to him, but couldn't make out what he was saying. The noise from the truck and the road more than filled his ears. Holding onto the side racks of the truck he managed to move closer to him.

"If Jaime has to stay in the hospital what are we going to do?" Jorge turned to look down the road for a moment, saying nothing. Then he leaned over so Bill could hear him.

"I have a cousin, we can stay with him if we need to." That seemed like the answer to everything for Jorge, but Bill still felt apprehensive. He consoled himself thinking that the old man was a local; he must know what he is doing.

The truck would move along at a good rate of speed, then slow down, hit a few holes, and then speed up again. It hadn't rained for a few days. This prompted the tires to hurl clouds of dust off to the sides as well as to the rear of the truck. At strategic spots people were standing along the road where a trail ended from back in the growth of trees. They stood their ground, hardly moving while the dust clouds raised by Nicolás settled around them. Some of the women covered their faces with a cloth.

As they drew closer to Puerto Ángeles they came upon a bus traveling the same route to town. Nicolás certainly wasn't going to allow it to be in front of him. He had to pass it even if it meant risking an accident. The truck shook and bounced as it hit every hole possible in the road, plowing through the dust thrown up by the bus. When the two were side-by-side Bill could see that the bus was loaded with passengers and cargo. On the roof there were bundles, sacks, boxes, even a restrained pig that was sticking its head out of a burlap sack, its eyes reflecting the amazed terror at the movement, noise, dust. All was secured in its place, and hopefully would stay there for the duration of the trip. Inside, the passengers too many for comfort or safety, stared out the windows at the passing truck. Jorge and his visitor stared back. The bus soon admitted it was no match for the new truck.

Conceding its defeat it slowed down and allowed Nicolás to pass. Slowing down even more, it sought to escape the dust the truck was tossing in the air. Slowing down, slower, it was soon left far behind. Unfortunately, Nicolás did not intend to improve his driving etiquette after this exercise in foolishness. This became apparent as the truck approached a village near the road.

The stop for the village of Santa Ana was located where the road came straight down a hill and then passed over a newly built large concrete bridge, which looked conspicuously out of place. A European nation had donated money for improvement of the country's infrastructure, and bridges were a high priority on the list of improvements. They were marvels of engineering that withstood the swollen rivers in the rainy season. However, there was one detail missing. No one seemed to remember that roads connect the bridges. When the floods came the bridges became islands in the midst of the rampaging waters, while the poorly made and maintained roads vanished, washed away by the deluge.

On the far side of the bridge where the terrain leveled out, an area cleared of trees and bushes had gradually taken form from the movement of buses and people. Here, vehicles could stop and let off, or take on passengers. The village of Santa Ana lay 400 yards further back from the road. This area was the social hot spot, where locals would congregate to talk, and hopefully find someone who would buy the products offered.

Booths and palm frond huts were erected as shelters for women who made *tortillas*, fried fish or sold peeled oranges. When a bus or a truck would stop women and children immediately surrounded it, like ants on a sugar cube. The scene would become hectic as they all clamored, screaming out what it was they were selling and the price they asked.

Some passengers tried to get off, others fighting to get on, luggage and personal property being lowered from or lifted into place on the roof. The passengers inside would stretch out their hands from within the bus, grabbing bags of this, or that, money being exchanged through the windows. Invariably the bus would start rolling while someone was passing the money to a vendor for the purchase of an orange. The coin would be tossed from the window as a last resort in payment. When the coin fell to the ground it resulted in a tussle amongst the boys to see who would keep it. This was commerce Santa Ana style.

Coming over the hill, Nicolás saw a bus stopped on the right side up ahead of him. Along with those selling their wares there were individuals milling about in the middle of the road, as well as some chickens from the village. Also, an occasional stray dog crossing back and forth, searching out something forgotten that could be eaten. Intent on putting a little excitement into their mundane life Nicolás began to accelerate, pushing even harder on the gas pedal. He observed faithfully his first rule of driving-he didn't use his brakes- just the horn. Looking down the road from the back of the truck Bill could see the coming confrontation.

"What is he doing? We will never clear all the people, not at this speed." Jorge heard the alarmed statement and fully agreed with it. The truck shook, the sides rattling, and dust was launched into the air from the speeding tires. With the horn blowing out an insistent warning, people began to scatter while parents plucked up their children. A defiant dog stood his ground in the middle of the road. He soon thought it wiser to move, apparently remembering what bravery had accomplished for others of his species.

The speeding machine roared passed the bus, the people, the dogs and the small huts set up by the women vendors. By some miracle, nothing was destroyed, nothing hit. That is, with the exception of one lone chicken who had unsuccessfully tried to evade the trucks front bumper. Peering through the cloud of dust behind them, Bill could see a few feathers floating about gently in the air as they drifted towards the ground. He also glimpsed in the swirl of the dust the gestures of some men who had been standing around the bus. They apparently did not appreciate the exhibition of Nicolás' driving skills. He of course loved it. He had a perfect excuse to do just what he had wanted to do for some time.

Having passed the bridge and the area of Santa Ana the truck slowed as the ever-present potholes began to appear in various spots of the road. Looking through the glass at the back of the truck's cab Bill could see Nicolás laughing with obvious pleasure. The man who was accompanying him joined in as any sycophant would, he knew who provided work, and who paid the wages.

After what seemed to be too long a trip the truck and its passengers arrived at the outskirts of Puerto Ángeles. There was a large concrete bridge spanning the river just southeast of town. The smooth concrete surface provided a welcome relief from the bumps and jolts received on the dirt road.

Below the bridge on either side, women washed clothes in the river. Children ran back and forth between hanging the washed items on nearby bushes to dry, and playing in the water. A few men were using the river as a car wash. They parked their pick-up trucks part way in the river and used the abundant water source freely.

The buildings of Puerto Ángeles raised their roofs above the palm and Guanacaste trees. The town always seemed much larger than it was when arriving from one of the villages.

Nicolás followed the road to where it turned off in the middle of town and drove with a measure of Sanity for a change.

Puerto Ángeles boasted a population of around eighty thousand, so his driving had to reflect a bit more caution. It was the largest town in this part of the country, there were stores, schools, a little of everything. The hospital was of course the largest in the area, not the best, yet it was better than nothing. It attracted people from the interior coastal region and up the coastline to the border. There was an international airport, the same one where a few days' before Bill had arrived. It was international in the sense that twice a week a flight left for the capital, and from there passage could be booked out of the country. The military also used the airport as home base for its antiquated jet planes that had been sent as cultural assistance from abroad. The main economic plus for the city was the port from which bananas, pineapples, coconuts and tropical wood were shipped to foreign markets.

The truck and its passengers came down a street lined by palm trees and drove between two cement pillars that marked the entrance into the center of town. When Jorge saw them he began to work his way around the truck box holding onto the sides. He knew the hospital was close by, so he was ready to get out the minute it came to a halt and the brakes had been applied. He climbed down with difficulty having stiffened some after standing for so long.

"I'll talk to the Doctor." Nicolás and his hired man walked around just as Jorge was on his way. "I am going to talk to the Doctor, I'll be right back."

"We'll be here, no problem go on." The hired man readily shook his head in agreement.

"How is the boy?" Bill was trying to flatten his wind-blown hair that stood on end. He moved over next to the hammock and studied Jaime in his suspended world. He didn't quite know what to answer. There were small bloody blisters around the area where he had been bitten. The swelling limb looked even more repulsive and there was a spreading rash.

"I guess he is doing as well as can be expected but, he doesn't look good." Nicolás said nothing for a moment.

"It is a miracle that he is still alive. I have seen grown men who didn't last this long. It all depends on the situation, how big the snake is. How much venom it has, where it bites you. You know what I mean." Again the hired man agreed fully to what Nicolás had said.

"Yeah, I hope he makes it. Jorge will... well, I think he will be fine, we got him here to the hospital." Bill was trying to convince himself.

The situation didn't seem to affect Nicolás that much. The boy wasn't his, and he didn't stand to lose anything if he did die. He easily turned the conversation to other matters.

"I heard that your father used to work for the company." Inés, being the center of the gossip hub in San Juan had informed her husband about the visitor.

"Yes, he worked for several years with the company. Did you know him?"

"Oh yeah, the agronomist Walker, we worked together quite a few times. I was a lot younger then."

They had worked together on several occasions, but it was not to the liking of Nicolás. Bill's father had obliged him to work, instead of letting him evade soiling his hands. He had a penchant for working as little as possible, while making you believe that he had done all he could. The father had not cared much for Nicolás, and that was a detail that Nicolás didn't wish to share with Bill.

"I suppose your father never made mention of me? My name is Nicolás Leva."

"No, I don't recall him saying anything about you, sorry." He felt that his comment had not been too complementary, so he sought to soften it.

"He worked with a lot of people and it would have been impossible to make mention of all of them."

For Nicolás it was far from unflattering. The lack of knowledge was comforting as it allowed him to weave the details into a more suitable cloak for him to hide behind. Bill found it awkward to not introduce himself formally. True, Jorge had not spoken well of the man, but up until now, the visitor hadn't even talked with him. He stepped around the hammock and walked to the back of the truck.

"It's a pleasure." He stretched out his hand as he spoke.

"No, the pleasure is mine." Nicolás smiled broadly revealing his two gold teeth.

He was just at the point of asking some more important questions like; what was he doing in San Juan, and more importantly, why had he gone out to camp nine? Abruptly, footsteps and animated voices alerted him to the return of Jorge with some of the hospital staff.

"Here is the Doctor." Jorge didn't have to say who he was. His white shoes, smock, and white pants made it obvious that he worked in the hospital. The physician moved rapidly and authoritatively so as to study the hammock and the boy. He directed himself to Jorge.

"*Señor* Valladares, does your boy have any wounds, broken bones? Did he fall after or before being bitten?"

"No, I don't think anything else happened to him. The snake bit him when they were playing by the river. No, he has nothing else wrong, just the bite."

"Fine then. We need to get him out of the hammock and onto this stretcher." The Doctor instructed the two men, hospital staff personnel that accompanied him, to place it on the edge of the truck bed. Nicolás ordered his hired man up into the truck to help Bill. They lifted the boy and placed him carefully on the stretcher.

"Get a firm grip on the stretcher. Watch his leg!" Jorge trying to move it with gentleness laid it next to the other and then let out a deep breath.

"You're at the hospital now son. You are going to be fine." No sooner had he said that than a light stream of blood began to run from the boy's nose marking a crimson path across his upper lip. Bill's face was drained of color as he saw what Jorge had warned of. Nicolás shoved his hat back on his head.

"Well, it's started. You better get your boy in there fast Jorge." As the words left his mouth, the Doctor had already reacted to the situation.

"Come along, let's get him inside!" The two men carried the stretcher with the rest of them behind, all except Nicolas' hired man who stayed behind to watch the truck.

They entered the hospital by means of a long corridor, and immediately the characteristic smell of chemical cleaners filled their noses. The Doctor conducted them to a room some fifteen by twelve feet. It had the usual high ceiling construction of tropical countries. The elevated ceiling helped keep the room cooler. A large fan slowly churned the humid, thick air but did little to clear the room of the smell of antiseptic. They laid the boy on an examination table.

"When was your son bit?"

"Early this morning."

"How much does he weigh?"

"I don't know exactly." The words did not come easily to Jorge

"Are you sure it was a *Barba Amarilla* that bit him?"

"Of course. I have seen them many times." A nurse began to cut away the boys pants. The Doctor, still bent over the boy raised his eyes from the leg, .

"You gentlemen can wait outside in the corridor." Bill was pleased with the idea; his stomach was beginning to feel the effects of the antiseptic in the air. Jorge looked like he wanted to stay, but, Bill kindly took his arm in one hand and gave him a gentle tug towards the door. The old man moistened his lips.

"We will be right outside the door." The Doctor acknowledged the father's comment with a nod of his head.

They stepped outside the room and found a bench in the corridor. They didn't say much. Jorge knew that nothing could be said. Nicolás had nothing of value to say. As for Bill, he didn't know what to say, so he began to look around, studying the hospital and its details.

It was built in the Spanish colonial style, with wide corridors and a high ceiling. Through the decades it had served several functions, ranging from political headquarters to military barracks. Bullet marks in the walls, covered now with white paint, indicated the building was a stronghold for revolutionary forces during one or more of the frequent civil wars. The medical attention that was provided in the hospital was partially subsidized by the government. The current economic situation in the country didn't allow for the best, or the latest, sometimes not even what was adequate.

From the bench he could see the entire open courtyard, around which ran a corridor, or covered walkway on all four sides. Patients were wandering about. One group was congregated trying to console one another. Others limped arduously, or drug a stiff leg painfully. A few supported themselves on crutches. They wore wrinkled smocks that had originally been white, now somewhat yellowed with age, and all stained. An old man shuffled by slowly. He raised his head, gazing dispassionately at the strangers through bilious eyes that had ceased to focus clearly.

Long dormitory like rooms containing 40 beds each opened out onto the courtyard. The beds were nothing more than metal frames covered by peeling white paint. Thin, damp, foul smelling mattresses stretched out on them. Several of the patients were sitting on their beds; others were lying pitifully in what would be there last home. A sign over the entrance to one dormitory read, "Men."

He decided to look away seeking something more positive to fix his eyes on. However, it was to no avail. Not far away a man was sitting in an antiquated wheel chair, its rubber tires worn off in several places. His family had brought him to the hospital seeking help. Bill gathered that he was the grandfather, possibly an older uncle. Whoever he was he had obviously traversed many miles in his life. His head had been shaved but now sprouted stiff bristles of mixed gray and white hair.

A doctor of short stature conversed with the family. He held a cigarette with great flair and elegance in one hand. In the other, he had a felt tip pin with which he was drawing on the patients head, marking out the route he was proposing to take in an upcoming surgery.

It took little for Bill to appreciate that this was no place for a sick person. The reality of life and death, suffering, arrogance, the impotence he felt in the face of such adversity, he had to say something, anything, he needed to get his mind pointed in another direction.

"Jorge, what are you going to do now?" The anxious father looked up, his cheeks showing clearly where his hands had been supporting his head.

"What do you mean? I am going to wait here to see what the Doctor says about Jaime." It was obvious to Jorge what he had to do.

"No, that isn't what I mean. I wanted to know what you are going to do with Jaime once the doctor gets done with him. Is he going to stay here?" The old man looked studiously at what was to be seen of the hospital from his position.

"You aren't going to leave him here, are you?" Bill had forgotten that this was the hospital, the place they had brought the boy to. This was all that men like Jorge had.

"What if he has to stay a few days?" Jorge let out a heavy breath.

"I can go see my cousin Alfonso, he lives here. I'll stay there until the boy is well enough to travel in the train back to San Juan." No one mentioned that the boy might not be going home. Jorge looked inquisitively at his visitor.

"What about you? What do you want to do?" He felt uncomfortably out of place thinking about the question. The acceptance that he had enjoyed at the Valladares home, owed to the personage of his father, was now awkwardly missing. He didn't have his papers, no clothes, and no money. Leaving to go back to San Juan was abandoning Jorge, and he needed him. What could he do anyway, even if he went back to San Juan?

"Well, I really don't know. I don't have anything here and, yet, I don't want to leave you. Maybe I can help out with something. Nicolás added his thoughts.

"Listen, if you want, I can go back to San Juan and have Santiago come tomorrow with whatever you need from home." His comment, rather than being a sudden display of concern and desire to help, was born more of a wish to leave behind the hospital and the present company. On the other side of town there were places more to his liking, and he wished to avail himself of them prior to his trip back home.

Bill offered his comment.

"Do you want me to stay here with you? Like Nicolás said, Santiago can bring us what we need?" The boy's father couldn't hide his pleasure at the thought. Having a foreigner as a friend, just made the situation seem more positive.

"Would you do that for us?"

"Sure I would, what else is there to do." Considering his options there wasn't anything else. As far as Nicolás was concerned arrangements had been made so he stood up.

"Well then, you don't need me here anymore. What would you like me to send with Santiago tomorrow?

Jorge felt that he needed little if anything, except the money that they had received from a hog he had sold some time back. He would certainly need the money, and his son could bring that.

The backpack that Bill had left in San Juan contained everything he would need, so that could be brought. Bill tried to impress Nicolás with the detail that he wouldn't wish to lose anything from the pack, so the boy had to be very careful traveling with it. Placing his hand on Jorge's back Nicolás offered his consolation.

"Don't worry old man, the boy is going to be fine. I will send Santiago on his way tomorrow in the bus." Then he added in a rather burdened way, as one who is very important would say.

"Off course, he will have to walk out to the road to catch the bus into town. I will have a good deal to catch up on once I get back, and I wouldn't be able to give him a ride out to Las Palmas where the bus stops. But, being young, what is an hour of walking. Oh, and by the way, don't you start worrying about how you will pay me for bringing you into town. We can settle the matter later on." Jorge knew full well that the debt would not be forgotten. He bowed his head slightly, acknowledging his obliged gratitude.

Unlike some of the *campesinos*, Jorge had not been conditioned to recognize his position in society as others had. The poor usually do not question, they do not protest, they merely accept their lot in life, and allow themselves to be herded wherever those with money and power wish to direct them.

His age and experience helped mask the disgust he felt for Nicolás. After all, he had brought them, and the boy was in the hospital now, that is what was of importance. Jorge couldn't help thinking what a mercenary, what a parasite his neighbor was.

In short order Nicolás was gone, leaving rather hurriedly when once a decision had been reached. He maneuvered his way around the patients and then down the corridor vanishing from view.

Jorge had begun to show the emotional and physical strain on his face. The lines seemed deeper, and his eyes sadder with less of the sparkle that they had held when Bill first met him. The two sat on the bench accompanied by their thoughts. They didn't say anything to each other for some time.

An opening door drew the attention of both. It was the room where they had left the boy. As it opened wide a man clothed in a white coat stepped out. Jorge noted that it was not the same doctor they had left Jaime with.

"*Señor* Valladares?"

"Yes, here I am." He rose to his feet as fast as he could.

"Well, be thankful, you could have lost your boy." He didn't quite understand the statement. As the words began to form a coherent statement in his mind, he deciphered them to mean that his boy would get better.

"You mean he is going to be all right, isn't that what you mean Doctor?"

"Yes, he will make it, at least, I think he will, but, he still is in a bad way and he is going to have to stay here so we can watch for infections, reactions and so forth. A problem with the venom of a *Barba* is necrosis." Jorge didn't understand the word necrosis, but he shook his head in agreement.

The Doctor motioned with his hand.

"You will need to go to the front desk at the entrance, right down that corridor and obtain the admittance papers." Bill found the Doctor's attitude rather matter of fact, lacking concern.

The foreigner didn't appreciate that the physician had become inured to suffering, death, the pitiful state of those he treated. Too many of the patients never recovered fully. The high rate of infections in the tropics, the lack of hygiene, the usual postponing of seeking medical care until the wound was a malodorous swelling or the condition too painful to endure, it all led to seeking too much, too late. With little modern equipment, the lack of drugs, and patients that didn't know how to cooperate with their bodies healing abilities, doctors at the public hospital had learned to preserve their own sanity by a dispassionate mental state of indifference.

While he had been talking with Jorge the Doctor had been filling out some forms on a clipboard.

"Here! Present this at the desk and the nurse will tell you what you need to do, and who you should speak with." Jorge received the form in his hand and the doctor turned and disappeared. The comments had brightened the face of the old man. He took Bill by the arm.

"Come on, we will talk to the woman about the papers."

Paper work is especially frustrating when you are tired and when your emotions are frayed. However, the two waded through the forms and took the appropriate cards back to the room where they had left Jaime. The door was open and no one was inside the room, that is, no one except a young man who was a medical student working at the hospital. He was cleaning up, gathering what had been left after attending to the boy. The two entered and the young man turned around facing them.

"Excuse me. Do you know where they took my boy?" He was bitten by a *Barba*, we had brought him here to the hospital." The nervous concern was evident by the rapid avalanche of information that was descending upon the young attendant.

"The boy, oh yes, are you his father?" Bill noted an air of kindness about the young man. He was probably new to the hospital job and pleased in thinking about his future career in medicine.

"Yes, he is my boy. Can you tell me where he is?"

"Well, I think Doctor Zúñiga had him taken to section 14." He walked over towards the door and pointed. "There, you see the sign over the entrance?"

"Thank you, thank you very much." The two stepped out into the open courtyard again.

"Don't be too worried about the boy. I heard Doctor Zúñiga say that he had seen worse." Jorge and Bill turned to hear the comment from the young man. He could see that his words hadn't been entirely caught by their ears.

"I said not to worry too much. I think your boy is going to be fine."

"Many thanks. May God hear you!" Jorge's steps came somewhat faster as he moved in the direction of section 14 where they had taken his son.

Bill continued to catch glances of people staring at him. He felt conspicuous, and rightly so. He was reminded why when he saw his reflection in one of the few windows. In it he saw the image of a man, his hair still showing signs of having been tortured by the wind, and his stature higher than the rest, definitely out of place. There were patient's images as well. Shadowy reflections, macabre images of men that didn't reveal the pain and hopelessness they suffered. They were short figures, dressed in hospital gowns that filled out their reflections like ghostly apparitions in some late night nightmare.

Two doors swung back and blocked by some large bricks opened up into section 14. A long room of 100 feet or so by 30 feet was before them. Beds lined both sides of the room, being close to each other obviously to accommodate as many as possible. Though the doors opened up into the courtyard the air suffered for freshness, which no doubt did not brighten the mood of the patients who lay on top of coarsely woven sheets marred by permanent stains. Little Jaime, laying listlessly was one of those unfortunate enough to be in the hospital.

When they came up next to the bed, Jorge doing so hurriedly, but with awareness that he was approaching a sick person, they could see that Jaime's arms twitched periodically. He was still asleep, or not asleep, but medicated, or then again maybe it was the poison's affect on him. Jorge didn't know all the details of his son's condition. He could see the small face of his little boy surrounded by a thin pillow.

"*Señor* Valladares." It was a subdued authoritative voice that called to them from behind. When Jorge turned he saw Doctor Zúñiga. The Doctor motioned with his hand to step away from the bed. Jorge remembered the cards he had in his hand that he was to give to the Doctor.

"Here are the cards the secretary gave us at the desk. I filled them out like we were told to do." Doctor Zúñiga took them and began to look them over. He then attached them to a clipboard that hung at the end of Jaime's bed.

"Thank you for filling them out. Will you be staying here in town?"

"Yes, I have some relatives that I will be staying with." He glanced back at his boy. "How long do you think he will be staying here?"

"That is hard to say. He's young. That gives him an advantage. But, he is small, and thankfully it seems the snake hadn't injected a good deal of venom. Otherwise, I don't believe he would be alive. We will know more in a day or two as we see how he reacts to the treatment, resultant infections, and other items that we will monitor. Stop by tomorrow to check on him. The best thing now is to let his body do just what his body is doing. So, look for me when you come." He left as quickly as he had entered.

The two lingered at the bedside for some time. Finally, Jorge told Bill that it was best they go to his cousin's house and see about staying with his family. Before leaving, Jorge used part of the sheet covering the boy to wipe the sweat from Jaime's forehead.

"You sleep well my son. I will be back later." Looking at Bill he managed a worried smile. They began to walk towards the courtyard. When they came to the door, Jorge stopped. Turning around, he looked back at his boy once more before leaving.

Chapter 7
Alfonso`s

Time seemed motionless at Alfonso's where Bill and Jorge were making the best of the situation. The cousin had warmly accepted the two into his home, in fact, the presence of the foreigner as a guest had made Alfonso quite a celebrity amongst his neighbors. It wasn't long before they were casually stopping by, or, pausing in front of the house long enough to be seen and then greeted. Then they would inquire as to who was the stranger. Some were satisfied with the answer that he was a friend of Alfonso's cousin; others preferred to believe their own conclusions on what was taking place.

Twice a day, in the early morning and then again just before sunset, Jorge would trek off to the hospital accompanied by someone from the family. Four days had gone by. It was obvious now that barring some unforeseen complication or infection the boy was going to survive. True, he would have a good deal of numbness in the leg for some time, and no one knew what he would catch or come down with from being in the hospital. But, the situation seemed positive.

Santiago had brought the items that would be needed by his Father and Bill while they stayed with Alfonso and his family. Reina, who remained at home, waited for news everyday on how her son was progressing.

Wishing to console his wife the best he could, Jorge had twice stopped by the local radio station. He left a message to be passed on to her over the air. This was the customary form of communication between those in town and family or friends in remote villages. An individual could stop at the radio station, where for a small fee their messages would be passed over the air at a certain time of the day. It was an electronic bulletin board, and the only way to communicate with those back home without someone going there personally.

Unadorned statements were broadcast to those who awaited news. Sometimes it dealt with sick members of the family, or, when they were to expect someone coming by bus that would need to be met with a horse or *burro* to help carry the goods they were bringing. Usually for the DJ it was a monotonous review of what he had before his eyes on the paper.

"Here we have a message for Genobeba from Carlos Bermúdez- '"Little Samuel is sicker than we thought, and the Doctor says he may die. I will be staying with my Grandmother at Poncho's for a few days.' "

"Here is a message for Don Alfredo, in El Portal- '"Concepción sold the pig and will be buying the things needed. But, she won't be able to come back until Friday on the bus. She wants you to bring the horse to pick her up down at the road.'" Then the DJ added:

"But, no need to bring a hat or a horse for the pig as he is staying in town." The DJ would sometimes liven up the message with a bit of humor, if the message allowed it.

Reina listened attentively everyday at the hour when they read the messages, awaiting news of her boy. After hearing one message about someone who had been in a wreck and wouldn't return home when they were expecting him, Reina's ears picked up as the D.J. read out the following.

"This message is for Doña Reina Valladares in San Juan from her husband Jorge; '"don't worry Jaime is going to be fine. We are staying at Alfonso´s and will be here for about another week. We will get home as soon as we can.'"

Everyone who had the radio on would hear the message. If you lived in a village with a few neighbors who also were listening to the bulletin, you could count on each of them coming around to tell you what you had heard for yourself. Then they would expect you to thank them profusely for the kindness of informing you.

The most entertaining messages were the ones that the individuals themselves were able to convey. If they showed up at the station when the electronic bulletin board was being aired, the D. J. would have them present their own message.

The radio announcer displayed a preference for young girls around fifteen years old. He knew that they would panic when they had the microphone in front of them. It was a terrifying experience for the rural girls who couldn't look a person in the eyes, or speak above a whisper for their disproportionate shyness.

"O.K." The DJ would say. "Here we have, what did you say your name is?"

"Who me? I am..." There would be a great deal of stuttering, hesitancy, a clearing of the throat. The voice alternated between a deafening roar and an inaudible whisper as they nervously moved closer to the microphone or recoiled in terror. The DJ would try to move them back or forward as the situation merited.

They would pop their p's, and at times mutter a barely audible whimper as shyness took over.

"My name is Lupita."

"And what is your message Lupita?"

" Mamá, this is Lupita. I am going to stay with my aunt María because Uncle Leonardo is drinking too much, and, so don't worry because he was arrested and, so I went over to María's house, that is Aunt María and, she said, she said I could stay there. So here I am. I arrived here in Puerto Ángeles without any problems."

The comments by the announcer would cause a smile somewhere, but not for the family of Leonardo and Lupita. "Well, there you have it from Lupita for her loving mother. Don't worry mamá your Lupita is fine, and Uncle Leonardo is in the tank where he belongs."

With young Jaime improving all were in a more relaxed frame of mind. So, amongst all the coming and going to the hospital, Bill slipped away now and then to take a walking tour of Puerto Ángeles.

His rambling took him down to the wharf, where he saw a large freighter that was taking on a cargo of bananas and pineapples. He watched as hundreds of boxes would move along conveyor belts and then disappear into the hold of the large cargo ship. He decided to venture closer. A company guard stopped him and asked what he needed. Explaining that he was merely looking around, he was summarily dismissed as being an idle tourist, and told with no uncertainty that he wasn't allowed in the loading area. A little authority does interesting things to a person's concept of his importance. Bill excused himself and continued his walk on the other side of the wharf.

Since there was no bay in Puerto Ángeles the wharf jutted out into the open sea. Its sturdy construction no doubt had been a product of careful thought. It was built to withstand the pounding of waves that struck with unbelievable force during the hurricane season. Near the shore the water was not that deep, but continual dredging to accommodate the fruit freighters kept the docking area to an appropriate depth.

On the side of the wharf where Bill was walking two small fishing boats were lazily bobbing up and down, rolling, dipping and displaying the movement of the waves. He saw that the freighter didn't move at all. It was at ease, resting. Men scurried about its deck as well as the wharf filling the stomach of the metal beast with tons of fruit.

He steadied himself on one of the concrete pylons of the wharf that had been sunk deep into the bottom of the sea. His eyes followed the pylon down to the water line, and from there, its distorted form as it stretched through the clear blue-green water, deeper and deeper, until it lost clarity and meaning and disappeared altogether.

A diver accompanied by a man in a small canoe caught his attention. The two struggled with a large fish that the diver had managed to spear. Judging by the size of the fish, it had given both of them a chance to test their abilities. A fish that size could have wrapped the diver around one of the pylons, entangling him in his own line as it struggled to free itself from the spear. He wondered how long they had been tussling with the creature. It was now somewhat subdued and part way into the canoe. A sudden revival of strength and flexing of its tail threatened the small vessel with capsizing. One of the men beat furiously at its head with a club. They would eat well and make some money. But, they had earned it.

He soon lost interest in the wharf but didn't see any reason to return to Alfonso's yet. So he continued walking towards the street market, which was four blocks away.

When he arrived it was teeming with individuals buying, selling, stealing, gossiping, some doing nothing except watching. People sat at booths with their goods on display. The booths were covered with linen materials, or corrugated metal; others were exposed to the sun. Everyone seemed to be talking about something; even those who stood alone were talking. They moved their lips, engaged in conversation with themselves or imaginary companions of the past. Clothing, food, hardware, flowers; it could all be obtained here.

A man sat on the corner, his six iguanas for sale. They looked pathetically helpless with their legs tied behind them and mouths sewed shut, which saved the prospective customers from a nasty bite.

"You want to buy an iguana?"

"No, no thanks."

"Why not? Hey look, these are fat ones and I will give you a good price." A passing woman stopped, being more interested in Bill than the iguanas.

"What do you say, come on you have the money. I know you do." They were beautiful indeed.

He studied the iridescent green of the animals, the shape of its head, the fin that ran down its back. He couldn't imagine though eating a lizard if something better was at hand. In the wild they ran free, and furiously scurried about under a brilliant sun. However, their days of freedom had passed.

"No, no I am not interested in them."

Moving through the crowds he studied the different stalls and their products. A woman with freshly made cheese slowly moved a piece of cardboard she held. The movement of air kept the flies from landing on her product. Though at times she would be distracted by something happening in the street, and when she stopped fanning, the cheese would be speckled with black dots that descended in great hoards to take advantage of the moment's negligence.

Pineapples were piled in a heap, obviously the entire load of a truck. They had been unceremoniously dumped with little concern for organization or hygiene. Bananas as well suffered the same discarded state. There was no ceremony, no systematic arranging in a tasteful fashion, no soft paper or rubber mats to comfortably rest upon as they waited for shoppers. Rather an intertwined community of yellow. A few had already been smashed into a purée and had been separated from their friends in a small pile to the side.

Several times someone had grabbed him by the arm and tried to pull him into their stall. He was an unconvinced customer though, and the proprietors would soon see that they could not coerce or cajole him into a purchase.

The food stands attracted his attention. These were the businesses of some rather stout full-bosomed women. Each stall consisted of a table, two or three chairs, a small liquid gas burner and some pots. They had a very simple and functional arrangement.

The menu hardly varied from fried fish, beans and plantains. The smell of that ubiquitous elixir coffee was in the air and settled upon his nose with enticement. He knew better than drink it though. The source of the water was in question, and the hygiene of the stalls was not that consoling. The customers stood, or sat as they ate.

There was a group in particular that caught his attention. It was a collection of men who had been unloading sacks of cement. The entire lot of them looked like they may have been host to more than one virus or bacteria. They were enjoying a meal as best they could before returning to unloading more sacks.

The shipment of cement had arrived in a truck, and the sacks were being unloaded into a warehouse. The only men who would be willing to sling the heavy bags on their backs, walking them out of the truck and into the warehouse were the local drunks. Unfortunately, there were more than enough of them for such jobs. These pilgrims of the street, who journeyed from one *cantina* to another with devotion, were willing to do anything for the opportunity to obtain their one pressing desire. Today they even had enough for food.

As Bill came up closer to the group, he could see that none had bothered to wash himself, the cement powder being caked in spots on their body and clothing. Their hair, a mass of oily matted material. The smell was distinctive, and pungent. Since they lived basically on *Aguardiente*, an undiluted alcohol derived from sugar cane, the air took on a special character. Alcohol exuded from their pores and the odor was unmistakable. The rags they called clothes, shiny from sweat and grime that had never been removed, were wet with perspiration that had flowed in ample amounts from their bodies.

He paused for a moment to consider them, seeking to not make his curiosity obvious. How long would it be before they had large running sores on their backs from the lye in the cement? The raspy coughing indicated that they had breathed in more than enough of the powder unloading the truck, or, that tuberculosis already had them in its grip.

One of them took note of Bill's interest, and, for a moment, stopped his chewing and focused his attention upon the stranger. His eyes were yellow orbs crisscrossed by red lines in a quilt like pattern. Hairs sprouted here and there on his face covered with several scars left from knife fights. The grime darkened fingers of one hand held a tortilla wrapped around some refried beans. It must have taken him some seconds to focus his eyes clearly, or, for his brain to interpret what he was seeing. When he finally did, he spoke, his words being barely discernible. He held up a morsel with great difficulty, his arm swaying back and forth. He was not entirely sober. Bill couldn't be sure of the meaning of the words, but the gesture of the upraised hand clutching the food was easily understood.

Bill politely indicated his refusal of the offering, producing some slurred profanity from the man as to the ungrateful nature of *gringos.*

One of the men was bleeding from a small wound on his arm. It took little for Bill's mind to rapidly change to Jaime still in the hospital. He looked at his watch and thought it was best to head back to Alfonso's.

It wasn't difficult to find his way out of the maze of the market. As he past the last stalls he came out on the main street. From there it was a straight shot back to Jorge and his relatives.

Before he realized it he had walked the distance back and was standing in front of Alfonso's house. He had arrived, physically that is, his mind was still mulling over the scene of the men unloading the cement.

The total lack of purpose in their life had struck a responsive chord in him. They were after all somebody's sons, but who would claim them now. He raised his cheeks in a muffled sign of amusement, thinking of how that would make a good line for some country western song of sad despair and forlorn experience, 'I'm mama´s boy, but who wants me now?'

As he reached for the handle of the front door he could smell the inviting aroma of a meal being prepared.

"Well, food doesn't seem to be a problem here. Smells like onions."

When Jorge saw him he immediately brightened up and received him like a lost son.

"How was the walk?" He rose to his feet with difficulty, since he had fallen asleep in a chair and was just convincing himself that he was awake.

An animated conversation ensued, Bill having a few questions for the old man about what he had seen around the dock area and the market.

It wasn't long before Alfonso came into the middle of it all and let them know that his wife had just prepared something to eat. The meal was short in duration due to the appetite of the three men. Afterwards Alfonso, Jorge, and Bill sat and talked about nothing of great importance, just some basic items, which nonetheless kept the considerations civil and animated.

They discussed the matter of Jaime. It had been decided that when he came out of the hospital he could stay with Alfonso and his family until he was stronger. That seemed best for the boy's health, as he would be close to the doctor and the rest in town would do him good.

The train would be making its run to San Juan in the morning. Jorge and Bill planned to be on it. As could be expected, and as was considered appropriate, the father wanted to see his son before leaving. They decided to be at the hospital early enough to visit and say their reluctant good-bye. The father would explain that Alfonso and the family would be in everyday to see him, also he would be staying in town to rest and recuperate before returning home.

The morning came soon enough, there seemed to be a bit more rushing than normal as the train's schedule was never worthy of confidence, and a few items needed to be picked up at the hardware store after leaving the hospital. Alfonso's wife had prepared a small package with a few items she knew that Reina would prize back in San Juan.

The children were all up to see their visitors off, prompted not so much by propriety as by the novelty of it all. Having a visiting relative was reason for excitement. His bringing his foreign friend, well, that was something of which none of the children in the neighborhood could boast. Bragging rights would certainly be theirs for many days to come.

Though the two were looking forward to arriving back in San Juan, each for his own reason, there was a measure of sadness in parting company with Alfonso and his family. The final hugs were shared and the visitors started making their way towards the hospital. Jaime was waiting for his father's promised visit, which ended too soon for all, as they had to reach the train.

Several of the passengers on the train were acquaintances, or neighbors, and all had heard of the episode with the snake, so there was no lack of conversation during the trip home. Though he was part of the exchange of comments, Bill's mind was occupied with his purpose in being in San Juan. *La Doncella* was again calling him back.

Chapter 8
The Captain Of *La Doncella*

The family and neighbors greeted the arrival of the group as a highlight of the year's proceedings. Not one of the neighbors failed to stop in and inquire about the boy's situation. Jorge was busy reassuring Reina of their son's welfare and that soon, very soon, he would be back home with them. This was done in between Reina's providing the visiting neighbors with coffee and corn meal *rosquetas*, a customary kindness. It was also customary that the neighbors take advantage of the kindness.

Bill tried to fit in as best he could with the activities of the family. He spent some time splitting wood for the kitchen. Jorge was pleased with the gesture. Nicolás, in harmony with his supposed superiority within the social structure of San Juan didn't feel it was necessary that he personally visit the family, but he did send one of his hired men. It took very little time for the man to express the feelings of his employer. Yet, he was in no hurry when the coffee and corn meal *rosquetas* came his way.

The visiting and conversing didn't stop Bill's mind from returning to the falls and The Maiden. How was he going to get back to camp nine without raising unwanted questions? His anxiety grew into a disquieting apprehension that gave him no peace. He busied himself as best he could in order to distract his thoughts. Finally, Jorge offered some relief saying that a neighbor had invited him to help out with a matter.

Benedicto, who had been a friend for many years, was going to butcher a pig, and Jorge had agreed to help him with the project. Though he had not consulted with his guest he also offered the assistance of Bill.

Jorges visitor knew nothing about dispatching a pig. However, when he was informed of the assignment he readily agreed to help, whatever help he might be. The old man was pleased with the ready disposition that he displayed.

Jorge then began to describe, that is in between his notifying Reina and the children about Benedicto's invitation, how they were going to go about the matter. The more details that were added, the more Bill felt equally fascinated and repulsed at the same time. He tried to camouflage the brutal act with an intellectual covering, saying to himself that it was an insight into the culture of the area, its agrarian life.

Soon enough the two, accompanied by several children and a few of the neighbors, walked down the path leading to Benedicto's house, which wasn't far. It was located on the edge of the village, away from the beach, and closer to the rising slope at the back of San Juan.

As they approached his home a good deal of talking as well children's excited chattering was heard. A large gathering of neighbors stood around the area in back of the house, some giving their opinion on the fire, if enough wood had been placed on it or if enough wood was available. Others were thoughtfully considering the pig, which was oblivious of the reason for the festive spirit. When Benedicto saw Jorge he immediately let out a whoop of delight.

"Here comes the main man!" Jorge laughed and began to receive many greetings of respect from his neighbors.

"What do you mean? You have butchered more of these animals than I have." Benedicto did have a good deal of experience in the matter, as he was the unofficial butcher of the village. Yet, Jorge's age and standing amongst the neighbors required showing some deference to him.

Two girls in their mid teens stared unabashedly at Bill.

A sudden squeal came from the pen and everyone turned to see the pig. He was a large animal of some 250 pounds, and obviously would provide a good deal of food for the families.

The distraction of the shrill squeal was soon over and the conversations ensued again. Bill, who was studying everything thoughtfully, leaned towards Jorge to be sure he could be heard.

"That is a big animal. How are you going to kill him?" Jorge noticed the hesitation in Bill's voice. This caused his eyes to shine with humor as he thought of the timidity of his educated city friend.

"Oh, don't worry. I will show you." An unwillingness of spirit swept across Bill's face.

"You know, not only am I going to tell you how we are going to kill him, but you are going to help." Bill's expression inferred that suddenly he wasn't that desirous of playing a role in the upcoming drama.

Benedicto began to consult with Jorge and several of the men about the preparations of the affair. The children began to scamper about vying for the best positions by the fence. It was an event not to be missed, especially with the stranger playing a leading role.

With the rope in hand, which would be attached to one of the hind legs, Bill and two of the neighbors began the struggle with the unwilling pig. After securing the rope to the leg they rapidly attached the other end to a post that had been driven into the ground. The pig knew something was amiss. There was hardly any slack in the rope. No room for maneuvering. No escape route. Jorge raised the sledgehammer high into the air. The suspense was palpable. It fell with finality on the head of the restrained victim. There was no last minute call for clemency, no stay in the execution, no mercy. The verdict had been rendered and the deed had been carried out. The carnivores won the case.

Bill didn't hear the squeals from the children; he didn't see the wrinkled noses of the girls who displayed some expected displeasure at the occurrence. He was focused on the body lying on the ground, how it shook in defiance, its stiffened legs straight and trembling. A neighbor rapidly produced a knife to drain the animal of his life giving liquid.

Bill had played his part. He recalled the saying he heard at Alfonso's a few days back, when they, that is Jorge, Alfonso and himself, sat together in the yard and talked of people and places. Jorge had referred to a well-known proverb in the conversation:

"He who holds the hoof is just as guilty as he who kills the cow." Making the application to an acquaintance of theirs who hadn't actually committed a crime, but, he knew who did, and didn't stop him from doing it. Now Bill was a determined carnivore just like the rest.

A heavy hand grasped his shoulder firmly, and he heard Jorge's patriarchal voice congratulating him for his part. He had just experienced a rite of passage. He had participated in the kill for the good of the clan. He did like meat, but he had never thought out the process of what was involved. It all seemed so sterile, so innocuous. You enter a store and look over what was offered. You exchange some money for it. You take it home in a neat package. There was no thought given to what it meant for the animal. He noticed that several of the local men were eyeing him and then making comments amongst themselves.

"Well", he thought. "That's life. You want meat, it comes at a price."

The entire matter of dividing the carcass proceeded with precision. Soon the meat, the skin, bones, and anything else that could provide nourishment had been divided amongst several of the neighbors, each taking with them a share of the spoil. Jorge was rewarded with a rather large portion of a hind leg, which seemed to grow heavier on the way home, at least to Bill who carried it. Reina and the girls would be pleased when they saw what the family had received.

Arriving at the house they hung the hind leg on a hook nailed to a beam over the smoking fire of the kitchen. Jorge excused himself to wash away the evidence of the kill. Bill stretched out in one of the hammocks strung between the posts of the corridor. His arms and legs hung over the sides, his feet on the ground. The hammock gently swayed back and forth. He moved little; only one foot was kept occupied pushing on the ground periodically to keep the hammock in its rhythmic swing. A bothersome fly was reminded by the sudden swat of a hand that he was not a preferred guest. After cleaning up, Jorge joined his friend. With a bit of groaning and some heavy breaths of air being puffed about, he positioned himself in his own hammock.

"Reina!" He apparently hadn't been heard so he gave a little more volume to his voice.

"Reina!" This time his wife heard him call and came to the kitchen door asking him what he wanted.

"Can you bring Bill and I a cup of coffee please?" He looked over at his guest lying in the hammock

"You want one don't you Bill?" Pushing his feet against the ground he managed to sit up and look over.

"Yes, I think I will. I need something to wake me up and get me moving again."

Reina disappeared into the kitchen and sought out two cups and the other items for preparing the brew. The jar where she kept her freshly ground coffee was taken off of the shelf and she removed two large tablespoons of the granular powder placing them in the funnel sock that served as the strainer. With great care so as not to burn herself with the boiling water, she poured the liquid over the grounds at the bottom of the strainer. Her dark eyes watching carefully so that the sock might not fill up too much, nor that the coffee coming out of it spill over the edges of the cup. A large serving of sugar was stirred into each cup so that it took on the consistency of watered-down syrup

The steam rose from the mixture carrying an unmistakable scent out the door on the afternoon breeze. The first cup she placed into the hands of Bill reminding him that it was hot. Jorge sat up to receive his with pleasure, thanking his wife for her service. She said nothing. Her smile indicated that she was pleased that her husband was pleased.

The two men savored their coffee and said little, until Bill, anxious to return to what was of interest to him, looked for a way to bridge his conversation to the matter of the falls.

"How long do you think Jaime will stay in Puerto Ángeles?" The old man lowered his cup and brought his mind back to his boy at hearing the question.

"Oh, maybe two or three weeks, possibly a little longer. The stay will do him good, and besides, he may learn something from Alfonso and decide to open up his own store some day.

"You know Guillermo, I wish I could afford to send him and his brother, in fact all of the children to school and then to the university. They could be a lawyer, or a doctor, an engineer, maybe a teacher. Who knows what they could do? At least they would be somebody respected. But, life in this village is work and uncertainty. Possibly you may live long enough and have sufficient to survive on with your family. Not that work is bad, well, just not so much of it." He heaved a loud sigh. "I guess I am getting old."

"And *La Doncella*? What do you plan on doing about that?" Bill swallowed the last of his coffee at hearing that the matter had been broached. Sitting erect he rested the empty cup on his knee. He needed to sound as disinterested as possible and yet as desirous as permissible. So, carefully weighing his words he expressed himself.

"Well, I would like to go out there again. I still haven't found out if the story is true."

Jorge moved his lips about as if a hair in his nose had suddenly begun to attack him. Lying in his hammock he looked up towards the tiles on the corridor roof over their heads. Then, thoughtfully and in a rather somber tone he said.

"Yes, I imagine you do."

"Do you think you could get me a horse to ride out there tomorrow?" There was what seemed to be an interminable silence before he answered.

"Yes, I can get a horse for you. But, do you really think you should go? Possibly we are being shown that we don't need to be looking for *La Doncella's* gold, if it is there." The tone of the voice indicated the uneasiness of one who sees beyond the obvious. A meditative silence ensued as they each contemplated their feelings.

"Bill, did you eat well and have a roof over your head before you came here?" The question somewhat amused him.

"Sure, I had a good job and a comfortable life."

"Do you think that your life will be better when you have what you might find out there?" He gave thought to the implication.

"Just a few minutes ago Jorge, you said you wished you could do something so that your kids would have a better life. You can't do that unless you have money. Money is what makes life possible. Do you realize what it will mean if I find what I think is in the cave? And, not just for me. I want you to help me find it. When we do, then you will be able to send your children not only to the university, but to leave this village and move into a house like some of those we saw in Puerto Ángeles. You can buy a truck like the one Nicolás has. You can be somebody, Jorge. Somebody that people will respect, and not push around. A better life; that is what you will have if we find what we are looking for." With the hammock swaying back and forth the old patriarch ruminated on what had been said.

"A better life? Maybe I would have money, but would it be better? Nicolás has money. Yet, is he happy?

Does he have a better life than me? Sure he can buy land, trucks and cattle." He sat up in the hammock and looked at his guest.

"Bill, I am an old man. I may not be as smart as you about things that can be learned in books, but I have learned; well, I have learned that-." Bill sat waiting for the comment that the old man had to offer him. His expectation wasn't rewarded. Jorge, in a moment of reflection, felt he couldn't quite express his feelings and therefore thought it best to say nothing. The wrinkled face sprouted a smile and he fell back into his hammock with an audible grown. Enjoying a contented laugh he directed himself to his guest.

"Listen. When you find what your after, I want you to build me a house right in front of Nicolás' house so I can stare across at him. But build it up on posts because I want to look down on him for a while. Can you do that for me?"

The comment indicated that the tale of *La Doncella* had become just that, a tale, like many others he had heard through the years. The jovial flavor of the words indicated Bill still had a friend, and he could count on getting the horse the next day.

"I will build you two houses." Bill lay back with his hands behind his head. The two said nothing, swaying slightly in their hammocks to keep any flying creatures like flies or gnats disorientated.

"Yes, two big houses you will have." The old man laughed with reserved skepticism at the comment.

Morning came early the next day, or rather; it started early as Bill was in an expectant mood. The family prepared a horse for him, as well as providing sufficient information on which trail to take to get to the falls.

Both the horse and the saddle were not exactly what he had in mind. The breed was small and of a non-determined color. The saddle was far from the solid tooled leather seen at quality horse shows. Its rustic nature was practical rather than esthetic. A wood frame covered with a piece of dried cowhide, no frills.

Reina had prepared some food consisting of *tortillas* filled with beans and a bit of dried, white and extremely salty cheese. She had wrapped them carefully in a cloth towel set aside for just such a purpose.

"Here, you will need these sometime today."

"Thanks Reina." He felt the warmth of the food through the cloth, a pleasant sensation. With obvious appreciation for its coming purpose he placed it in his tote sack that had been strapped to the saddle. She saw it as being rather odd that he should go by himself, and her husband wasn't offering to go.

He took hold of the reins and prepared to swing himself up to mount the horse. It really wasn't much of a feat, considering that the horses of the area were not much larger than the *burros*. His leg caught momentarily on the small shovel he was taking. It took just a moment for him to free it. Yet, it was sufficient time for the action to draw the attention of the children and Reina, along with some of the neighbors who were watching from their houses. She knew better than to ask why he was carrying a shovel. Sometimes it is best to not know everything, or to be told in front of others that you don't need to know everything. He moved a little this way and that so as to accommodate himself in the saddle. Taking note that it wasn't going to be easy to find a comfortable position he resigned himself to the reality of the saddle.

"Well, I will see all of you later in the day."

"Wait, you are forgetting your *Cumbito!*" Santiago's reminder was appreciated. The dried gourd with a corncob stuck in its opening served as a canteen, it was his source of water. He could always drink from the streams and take the chance of amoebas, but he wished to forgo that experience if he could.

"Hey, I would have missed that. Thanks Santiago." He surveyed the field of faces. Jorge nodded with his head in a silent blessing. Reina softly stated;

"Be careful young friend."

He smiled, and then gently nudged the sides of the horse with his feet as he made a noise, which the beast understood to mean that it was time to move.

Riding out of the village a few men glanced his way. Some women stopped talking and fixed their eyes on him. He knew it was more curiosity than malice as they laughed when he reached a respectable distance.

The dirt road, a trail really, was where Jorge had said it was. With so few roads there was no confusion in finding it. The trail would avoid the lagoons and lead him to where he could easily ford the streams. Eventually, the trail would follow the rail line ending at where the *Burra* had been left the day Jaime had been bitten.

It was a peaceful setting, the horse doing all the work, and nothing left for him to do but think.

His mind readily drifted onto thoughts of the Spanish Captain with his soldiers. Could they have come through this same area? If they had, there would have been no roads, no houses, no San Juan. What would have been going through their mind?

Chapter 9
Left Behind

A madeus Rodrigo de Sevilla, Captain of *La Doncella de Belén*, master of one of his majesty's ships. Better to say, what had been one of his majesty's ships. Now, he was in command of three auxiliary boats, and the crewmembers who managed to escape with him from the sinking ship.

He had been entrusted with a shipment from the royal mines. It had crossed the Isthmus of Panama by pack animals, and his vessel was to see it safely to the Island of Hispaniola where he would join the treasure fleet heading for Spain.

Captain de Sevilla did not relish explaining how he had lost the ship and its cargo in a surprise evening attack by pirates, the type that preyed upon ships like his. The few men in the boats with him had eluded death in the struggle. One broadside from his crew produced a decisive explosion, bringing to an end the career of the pirate's vessel. The predator had become the prey and took little time in sinking, but, not before his ship had been severely damaged as well. The order to abandon *La Doncella* to the mercy of the sea had been given, though reluctantly.

In controlled panic the men that were not incapacitated by their wounds gathered what they could of food and water. They scurried over rigging and debris to get off before the vessel went down, taking them along with it. Those who were severely wounded with no chance of recovery were left to accompany the ship to its final resting place.

The boats were rowed a distance until the Captain gave the order to wait. All knew what to expect. The sea reflected like a mirror the light of the early evening, making the ships last moments visible. *La Doncella* left the surface world and was baptized into death. Every man's heart, though hardened by a sailor's life, sank with the comrades that had been left behind. No one spoke. Being aware of their own conduct both in private and in public, not one among them could say that he was a paragon of virtue. So, their thoughts naturally turned to their own mortality, and what might await them when light would cease to shine upon their faces.

Their priests had terrified them with tales of a coming retribution for the evil deeds they had done. It was a retribution in which some of the priests apparently did not truly believe, as their behavior was not in keeping with what they preached. But, that fact didn't eliminate the uneasiness or pangs of conscience.

That night as well as the next day passed with little to eat or drink. What was available was rationed and being made to last as long as it could.

By late afternoon the Captain raised a hand to shield his eyes from the sun as he scanned the horizon, peering with expectation for the first glimpse of mountains rising from the sea. An endless sheet of gently undulating water stretched before them into oblivion. He knew though that they were close to land so it was just a matter of time. Enduring hunger and thirst is just a matter of time as well. How long could they last in the boats? What did the future hold for him having lost the ship and its cargo? He glanced at the other boats and then nervously looked down at his feet. His thoughts centered more about what he would do when they did reach land, rather than what would happen if they didn't.

Nestled by his feet was a large sack. It contained some maps, papers, as well as another item, a metal chest, not large enough to attract attention, but sufficiently large to accommodate it's contents. That item made the sack heavier than what would be expected. Only he knew what that item was, and it would be best that the matter continued that way. He trusted some of his men, but not all of them.

It was on the third day when they began to see shore birds flying about, as well as vegetation such as limbs with green leaves that floated on the surface of the sea. Now, they knew they were getting close to land.

One of the crew finally saw what they had been searching for on the horizon. Mountaintops were slowly rising from the sea. With time the mountains began to join with a landmass that occupied the entire view to the West. They called out to one another as those who had defied death and lived to tell the tale. Despite festering wounds and thirst, their spirits rose with the rising of the mountains from the sea. The hours passed, and finally they came to land.

The boats were beached with difficulty, not because of the surf that was relatively calm, but rather the weakened condition of the men. Yet, amongst their suffering they saw as a fortuitous sign that a narrow river emptied into the sea near where they made land fall. Though they came from the sea, their priority was water, sweet water.

Moving cautiously at first, they were overcome by their desire for water and rushed towards the river. A pool had formed some yards inland before mixing with the sea, and though the Captain called for caution they plunged their faces into the precious liquid. This undisciplined exposure brought no evil with it, as unbeknown to the Captain and his men there was not a soul within many miles of their location.

Having calmed their thirst and dipped their heads again and again into the cool fresh water, they became more apprehensive of their security. Who might have taken notice of their landing?

The Captain organized his men, who with lethargy obeyed the orders.

They took up a position under some palm trees where they carefully checked their weapons to see if the powder was dry enough for the guns to be useful. Occupied with this inspection they continued to scan over as much of the area as they could from their position.

Satisfied that there was no immediate danger, the Captain sent some to gather coconuts that had fallen to the ground. Others began to attend to the wounds of their comrades. Night would soon be upon them and where they were on the beach was as good as any place it seemed. The boats were turned over and placed in such a way as to form a low wall behind which they took up posts. Some rested, others served as guards. Behind their fortress walls with their backs to the sea they enjoyed a measure of security. They began to eat the coconuts, stripping the husks from them with swords. It wasn't much, but for hungry men a simple item can be a banquet.

They continued preparing for the darkness that was approaching. The Captain gave what orders seemed appropriate and all began to accommodate themselves as best they could. The night held no surprises, though unfamiliar noises would startle the sentries periodically. It was the strange New World, but it was land, and for that they were grateful.

For the Captain a restless night lay ahead as he had a great deal to think about. He knew more or less where they were, and of a settlement, or outpost. But he couldn't enter it carrying what he had in the small metal chest. The ship was at the bottom with the cargo, how was he to explain the details so as to elude the blame for the loss of his ship and so many of the crew? A friend might be bribed, whereas an enemy would imprison him. That is why he decided to beach the boats where he did. Some of the men had served under him before. They began to encourage the rest telling them that soon the Captain would have them back with their countrymen.

He lifted his head sufficiently to look at the sack next to him. In it was an item that would provide nicely for him back in Spain. His pulse quickened as he recalled the day he first saw it. Guilt prompted him to forget the details of how it came into his possession. He consoled himself by remembering that it was a holy endeavor to separate the heathen from their idol worship? The means to do so were not of importance. It was a just cause sanctified by The Church. And if they didn't cooperate, well, they deserved their end, or so his priests had told him.

This twisted logic continued to seek the manner by which he could excuse his lack of ethics and morals. He recalled how the gold of the eight-inch statue glistened in the sun. But, the stone set in its middle! Yes, he never had dreamed that an emerald could be so big. It would be worth a ransom! The momentary joy turned to anxiety when he remembered his situation. A place must be found to hide the idol, and then he could return for it.

Morning comes early on the beach with the sun rising to greet the new day. Having nothing to shield them from the elements or the light of the morning, the men woke, stretched and shook off the stiffness of the night. The Captain was up, and stood looking out to sea. With grunts and grimaces the group began to organize itself, considering what the day was to hold. They attended to necessary activity upon rising, retrieving water, seeking out their meager allotment of food. The Captain had arrived at his decision on how to address the situation.

"Crew of *La Doncella*!" All heard the commanding voice of the Captain.

"We have a garrison in Puerto Ángeles, a settlement which I believe is not far from us. There, we can obtain the help we need. That being the case, I am going to take Francisco, Gabriel, and Arturo as well as a few others with me. We will take one of the boats and run up the coast until we come to the outpost. If all goes well we should return within seven to ten days. Felipe will be in charge until my return. I foresee no trouble for you here close to the beach. But, keep guards posted and be ready to defend yourselves. You can obtain water from the river, some of you will gather what is found to eat, you won't have a great deal, but you shouldn't starve either."

Bill could envision the men on the beach and the details of how the Captain, before he set out for the settlement, had left his men briefly and traveled inland following the river. He had gone by himself, informing the crew that he could move about more quietly being alone, seeking any potential danger for his men left behind on the beach. His crew saw this as an act of heroism, valor. He knew though what he would discreetly carry with him.

The trip upstream led him to a small cavity or cave at the foot of the mountain. There, he left his precious idol. With his sword he inscribed the words, "*La Doncella*."

He had planned to return and claim his treasure. But, his plan never materialized. Eventually he was imprisoned for the loss of the ship, and sent to Spain in chains where he not only lost his freedom and the riches he would have gained, but his sanity as well.

One of his sons became a low level bureaucrat, and as such had written a little known history of life in New Spain. In the account he commented on his father's misfortunes as well as the improbable ravings about his lost statue.

The family and friends of the Captain considered the matter as the wild dreams of a man driven into insanity by his confinement in prison, and possibly the result of a tropical fever. The son's account passed down through the years, to be shelved finally in the Library of Seville amongst thousands of documents and writings from and about the New World.

It was a minor detail, hardly believable. The son's reference was of no apparent interest. The Captain, who like millions of others, had been born, grew to maturity, died, and then was no more. The account would gather dust in the Library of the Indies, hardly noticed.

Bill would read it though, and he would see the tale echoed in the words of his father's diary. It would prompt him to seek what the master of *La Doncella* had left behind.

Chapter 10
The Tale

Bill was now a goodly distance from San Juan. The saddle didn't seem to annoy him as much as he felt it would. So, his mind was occupied with what he hoped was waiting for him. It was easy to imagine how he would simply ride to the falls, retrieve the statue, and then be on his way. However, he knew that such thoughts were simplistic, a far cry from what reality might require. Rather than frustrate himself any further with such thinking he decided to focus on the scenery.

The sun was shining through the patches of vegetation, and the easy rocking pace of the horse contributed to producing a serenity that was arresting. It resulted in a mitigating effect on worries. Yet, it wasn't long before negative thoughts sprouted without his prompting them.

"What if the Captain was really crazy, deranged? There might not be a statue. Then, why was the inscription by the waterfall, just as the Captain had said? No, the similarity in the details was not to be discounted."

The expectation of what awaited was almost unbearable as he could imagine the weight of the idol in his hands. His expectancy moved him to goad the horse into a faster pace, which brought him to camp nine in short order.

At the falls all was tranquil. No one had disturbed the peace of the setting. Dismounting from the horse, he tied the reins to a sturdy branch. Again, he stopped to listen. There was the sound of water tumbling over rocks as it pursued its course in the stream. A few birds were calling out territory boundaries, or seeking the attention of a willing partner to take up nesting. There was nothing to arouse concern.

Humming nervously his fingers untied the machete from the saddle. He and Jorge hadn't seen the cave. Yet, it had to be close by the inscription. He began to clear away the vegetation with the machete so he could clearly see the writing.

"Should I go to the right or to the left?" He started chopping to the right to find the opening to the cave. A distasteful memory of Jaime came upon him, sending a chill up his back. He stopped chopping momentarily and looked hesitantly down at his feet

"With all this noise I have probably scared away any snakes." He gripped the machete securely. A defiant spirit rose in him towards any viper that would dare stop his search.

He set to work the sweat pouring from his body. Swoosh! Swoosh! Swoosh! The machete sliced through the vegetation as the plants submitted to the blade.

At length the falling leaf-laden vines revealed an opening about 6 feet wide. It was a cave formed by water that over time had eroded the rock. In the distant past the streambed had changed its course, and the waterfall no longer was a factor in the characteristics of the cave.

"This is it, I have found it!" He could scarcely believe that he had actually come upon what he was looking for.

He vainly sought to control the delirious sensation of the moment, telling himself that the idol might not be there. Maybe someone had found it before, or, maybe the Captain hadn't left it. The effort at logically assessing the possibilities did not allay his excitement. His mouth was dry, not so much from the heat, rather from the nervous state he had worked himself into. He rushed back to the horse to retrieve a flashlight. The beast stood in the shade of the trees totally unimpressed by the activity.

At the mouth of the cave the beam of light barely made things visible. There was some growth of plants and moss at the entrance. He knew it would be wise to throw a rock or two inside, ascertaining if any snakes, or other creatures he would not wish to encounter had taken up residence. Three rocks were found quickly, and he tossed them one by one into the cave, listening carefully as each struck noisily against stone. There was no sound other than the rock striking other rock surfaces. No movement, nothing. Grasping the machete firmly with one hand and the flashlight with the other he stepped into the opening. It was musty smelling, the ceiling low. Adjusting to the darkness he could see that the cave didn't go back very far. He carefully examined the walls and the floor.

"Where would he have left it?" The Captain hadn't been specific about exactly where he had placed the small chest.

"It wouldn't seem logical for him to simply place it on the ground. Would he have buried it? No, I can't imagine that, but maybe he did."

The beam from the flashlight spread out along the walls forming shadows. To his left, close to where the cave ended and just above ground level, an area of rock jutted out. The light rested upon a form barely discernible that formed straight lines, partially hidden by moss.

"The chest!" The years and the humidity had formed a mass of rusted metal buried by debris, moss and earth, leaving only the lid exposed.

Excitedly, he cleared away what he could with the machete, searching where he might insert the blade to raise up one of the two rings serving as handles. It was useless. It refused his nudging. Raising his foot he kicked the chest, gently though, then in a more decisive manner. It moved. Somewhat reluctantly he placed the machete back in its scabbard, and then made an attempt to hold the flashlight in such a way that would enable him to take hold of the coffer.

Carrying the chest and at the same time trying to illuminate his way out of the cave proved to be somewhat difficult. Stumbling, he burst forth into the sunlight and then hurriedly moved towards the horse. A sudden onset of paranoia took hold of him. He turned, suspiciously analyzing every twig or limb moved by the wind. Once satisfied that no one had invaded the area, or was denying him the euphoric satisfaction he felt in this moment of triumph he placed the chest on the ground.

The lock, attached to the hasp was now a clump of rusted metal. He would have to use the shovel to pry or snap it off. Excitedly, he set to his task knowing that within a few moments he was going to be the only one to see what had been hidden for years. A strength born of desire flooded his body. He hit the lock again, and again, prying with the shovel until it finally submitted and lay broken. The chest had been damaged in the process, distorted, some of its rivets snapped. Now the moment! The rust though had sealed the box. The lid refused to cooperate. Grunting and grimacing, sweat running into his eyes, he searched for an opening to insert the blade of the shovel. A sudden snap of the oxidized metal sent the lid flying to the side. The idol stared at him shimmering brightly in the sun. He studied its upraised arms, the exquisitely formed nose, and the large drooping ears. The only distraction from the unmarred beauty of the gold was the opaque green of the unusually large emerald mounted in the figurine's middle. Stunned, he couldn't move for several minutes.

"I can't believe it. It was actually here."

The horse, swishing its tail, scattered some harassing bugs. Bill heard nothing, and was aware of very little as he studied the figure before him.

"What a beautiful piece of work, real museum quality." His fingers ran over the smoothness of the gold.

"No wonder the Captain picked this one to take back to Spain. He would have been a rich man." His insecurity grew as he contemplated his prize.

"I have to get this put away and get back to San Juan." A thousand details now flooded through his mind all in disarray and jumping from one point to another. Where would he put it? What will Jorge think? How to get it out of the country? With much tenderness he lifted it from the box with both of his hands, the same way a nursing mother would have raised her newborn infant from its cradle.

A snapping limb brought his stomach up to his mouth. He immediately turned clutching the figurine close to him. No one was there, just the wind rustling the leaves and the branches, just the wind. Though it was day he felt a sudden chill pass over him. His eyes scanned the area suspicious of every movement. Satisfied that there was no threat he hurriedly retrieved a towel from the items that were still tied to the horse. With the towel in hand he carefully swaddled his precious idol with attentive concern. Then, it was placed ever so cautiously into the saddlebag.

The remnants of the metal box were hidden in the bushes, with little concern for its historic value. His professional feelings had been swept aside by the dream of wealth. No indication of what he had been doing at the falls would be left. The horse and the items he had brought, plus his new acquisition were all readied for a triumphant return to San Juan. The reins were loosened from the limb and he swung himself up onto the horse.

The opening to the cave was visible, though the chiseled letters were not easily seen. Anyone happening upon the cave would think it was just another crevice, and the letters if found, well, just a mystery as they had been for many years. With a gentle prod from his feet, and a few selected noises he encouraged the horse to seek out the trail again, its hoofs making dull thuds as they met the soft moist earth. The beast moved with indifference of the cargo it carried. It could not discern the difference between coffee and gold, but Bill did. He readjusted his position and the wooden frame of the saddle creaked under his weight. Other than these noises, everything was as it should be, nothing unusual, nothing of concern.

He spoke with the horse as he rode along. Yet, he did not allow himself to be so distracted by his thoughts that he would fail to consider every movement around him.

The sun was brighter. The vegetation was greener.

The air was so pure a person scarcely had to breathe to fill his lungs. Life could not be kinder to Bill than it was at this moment. He wanted to break into a gallop, run or cry-out at the top of his voice. Restraint was called for, he had to sit on his feelings and hold them down. No one was going to find out what he had, no one. The ride back was the longest short trip he had ever taken

Chapter 11
The Dilemma

Riding back to San Juan he had much to think about. Above all, he knew he couldn't create more questions about his activity than necessary. He had to be not too excited, just happy for having been in places that brought him memories of his father. Hopefully, there wouldn't be too many watching eyes.

Coming around the last turn he could see the village. Passing the first house a dog delegation came out to greet the horse and its rider. Their thin bodies couldn't handle too much excitement. Soon enough their choral barking ceased and they decided it best to retire to the shade of a large tree where they would forget the merriment of the moment.

The horse knew he was home. It manifested delighted approval by making restrained snorts as the air passed through its nostrils. The arrival didn't seem to give rise to any undue attention by the neighbors. In fact, it was rather subdued at this hour. Just a few women took notice of him, and they busied themselves in daily affairs of retrieving water, or hanging clothes to dry on the fence. The gate at the side of the house was open and he was able to guide the horse through the opening. The animal had done it many times before and didn't need any instructions from him.

Santiago was the only one home. He greeted Bill respectfully and offered to help remove the saddle.

Shifting his weight onto the right stirrup Bill lifted his left leg and dismounted. Once his feet were on the ground his hand moved rapidly to the saddle pouch, which he held in a tight grip while the saddle was removed.

"Where are your folks?"

"They are buying some things at *Don* Nicolás' store. They should be back soon. How was your trip to the falls?"

"Oh, it is beautiful. But, you know that." His comments were studied and controlled.

"To bad that more people can't enjoy what all of you have here."

Santiago would have gone to the falls with Bill, however, with what took place with his brother he knew better than ask his father for permission. The boy's father was unsettled still by how close he came to losing his son. He didn't blame the foreigner. However, it wouldn't have happened had they not been at the falls.

The saddle was placed over a fence for the moment. The horse buried its nose in a pail of water drinking deeply, swishing its tail from side to side to keep the flies at a distance.

Bill had gone into the house to place his treasure at the very bottom of his backpack. He covered it over with clothes, feeling relieved that it was in what he considered a reasonably safe place. He didn't hear the footsteps behind him.

"*Don* Guillermo." He jumped, scattering some of his socks in the process.

"Santiago. You really gave me a scare." He glanced at the backpack. Gathering the items he placed them inside. Though the boy hadn't meant to startle him, the reaction was worth a nervous laugh.

"Do you want a cup of coffee? My mom left some." The boy had been instructed to not neglect the guest if he came back before his parents returned..

"Yes, that sounds good. Can you get me a cup please?"

At the store Jorge and Reina had just walked out with the items they had purchased. Some bars of laundry soap, salt, palm oil shortening, and two blocks of dark raw sugar. The items purchased had found their way into the sack thrown over Jorge's shoulder for the return trip. To him it seemed almost comforting to feel the weight of the sack. He could still work, still walk. He had learned through the years that it was better to see his blessings rather than to lament his trials.

Reina's normal schedule would have found her attending to the daily details as a wife and mother. But, at this moment it was exhilarating to stroll with her companion of many years, enjoying the day together, and what a glorious day it was. The enamored couple was unaware of the fixed attention of Inés and Nicolás who watched them pass under some trees a short distance from the store.

"How much is he going to pay you for taking his boy to Puerto Ángeles? You know that if you don't tell him soon you won't get what you are entitled to." Long ago Nicolás had begun to ignore his wife when she spoke.

"Are you listening to me?"

"Yes, yes, now quit pestering me. I have some things to consider which are of more importance." An icy stare at his wife prompted her to shuffle her body to another part of the house, though it was done with obvious displeasure.

A different atmosphere existed in Jorge's house. Bill and Santiago were sitting under the shade of the corridor roof. The guest enjoyed his coffee with a restrained exuberance as he reflected on the details of what he had accomplished. He was oblivious to how Santiago was studying him carefully, his boots, his size, and the hair on his forearms. Finally becoming aware of the studious glances Bill fixed his eyes on the boy. Santiago immediately looked away with seeming indifference to the family's guest. The boy lifted his cup to his lips taking a draught of the liquid.

"So, what would you like to do in the future Santiago? Would you like to go to school, or would you rather keep living here in San Juan?"

"Oh me. Well, I think I would like to be an engineer." The comment made him display a rare moment of talkativeness, or, maybe the coffee was lifting his spirits.

"It wouldn't be easy I know. Because, I would have to go to the university, and it takes a lot of money to do that, to study I mean and, well my dad doesn't have much money. I might find work though." At Santiago's age everything seemed possible. He hadn't faced the injustice of the world, the perfidy of those who pulled the levers of society. Venturing his innermost thoughts and with a sincerity born of ignorance, he decided to pose a question he had wanted to ask for some time.

"*Don* Guillermo, is it true that everyone in your country is rich"? The young boy's innocent question elicited a laugh, which was a difficult task for Bill as he had a mouth full of coffee.

"Rich? No, not everyone is rich." He reflected a moment before continuing.

"There are plenty of poor people, maybe not as many as here, but just the same poverty exists everywhere." The boy's eyes widened as the visitor launched forth on an explanation of the inequalities that exist.

"The sad fact is there are poor people who don't have to be poor. There is enough for everyone, just that, well-." He was being forced to articulate a plausible reason for an unreasonable situation to a boy who dreamed of the future.

"Some people use other people to obtain power and money and they don't want to share either, but they want more power, and more money. Some people work hard and achieve their dream. That is what is amazing. You can do just about whatever you want. You don't have to be marginalized by those at the top. Economic barriers, social barriers, racial barriers they can all be overcome if you work hard. Well, usually you can. Unless your circumstances are not the best, or you run into the wrong group or some tragedy happens. Then you, well... well the thing is you can live your dream if you want to. Just don't let success change you. That is the challenge. Otherwise you become just like those who don't want others to succeed."

He had been looking off into the Distance when these last words crossed his lips. His eyes returned to Santiago who was sitting in a rhapsody of attention, not understanding fully but enthralled by Bill's discourse, which neither confirmed nor denied what the boy wished to believe.

The comments made Bill reflect on his own attitude. What would he be willing to do to obtain his dream? As he reflected on the course he was taking a wave of uneasiness invaded his convictions.

"It is probably best to think of what kind of a person you will be Santiago, and not worry about money so much." With a look of defeat painted on his face he drank the last of his coffee. Conscience is a wonderful faculty when it corrects our defects, but it is an implacable adversary when an individual tries to stifle it.

The sound of shuffling feet and a few associated noises of thankful-to-be home sounds announced the return of Jorge and Reina.

"Guillermito, you made it back early. That's good."

The voice of Reina put an end to the conversation between the visitor and the young boy. Jorge wearily dropped onto a leather-covered stool with a groan of delight at being able to sit. He rested his back against the wall. His wife took the sack from her husband and disappeared into the kitchen.

"Take it from me my friend you don't want to get old." This was one of those days when it seemed that he was growing old after all, though he made the statement with a smile. He pushed his hat back, leaving a sprouting of sweaty wet gray hair sticking to his forehead.

"Well, did you see what you wanted at the falls?"

"Beautiful, *Don* Jorge, just beautiful. It was just what I had hoped it would be." The old man gathered that he had found what he was seeking.

"Santiago, did you take care of the horse?"

"Yes, I did Papá." Jorge noticed the cup in his guest's hand.

"Looks like you gave him a cup of coffee too. Well done my boy! Why don't you go see if your mother needs some fire wood for the evening." The boy hurriedly rose to his feet and moved on to the assignment.

The two were left alone. Bill looked towards the kitchen. He wished to assure himself that what he was about to say would be heard only by Jorge.

"I found it! It was just like the Captain had said. You and my father had found the place where the statue was left."

"Where do you have it?" He thought that the old man would be more animated or excited about the news. He didn't answer immediately. Again he surveyed the area to make sure no one was listening in on the conversation.

"It's in my backpack."

"Good, no one will bother it there. Tell me, what do you plan on doing with it?" The question puzzled him.

"What do you mean? I am going to get it out of here. Back home I can sell it to a collector for a fortune." At this comment Jorge voiced a sound of disbelief.

"Do you think they will let you just walk through the airport and get on a plane without asking questions about your-whatever it is, statue, idol or the like?"

Bill knew that he was right. It would be impossible to pass through customs on both ends of the journey. The statue would be confiscated and he would be arrested. He was not a smuggler at heart. But, surely there was more to be gained by his selling it to some collector. His receiving a small percentage of its worth, or gathering a few plaudits from local politicians and the staff of some university for handing it over was not exactly what he had planned.

"Once you start lying, you will have to tell another lie, and then another. Soon enough you will be living a lie. Liars always look behind themselves. They don't sleep peacefully." The fatherly advice was meant well, and the young man knew that what he had been told was true. The straightforward exposé stung, but not deep enough.

"I found it, and so it is mine. I say I can do what I want with it." The tenor of this comment was out of harmony with his being a guest in Jorge's house.

"Yes, it is yours, just like it belonged to its owner, and then the Captain. Now it is yours. Will it profit you more to have it than it did them?" Jorge had seen the same look in the eyes of others. He knew what it drove men to do and what it compelled them to abandon.

Unaware of this conversation between the two, Nicolás was occupied with his own thoughts. He was meditating on what he had seen a few minutes prior. He had watched Jorge and Reina as they passed a large mango tree heading home. The obvious seasoned love they held for each other embittered him greatly. His head had turned towards the door through which his wife had disappeared. A long and laborious sigh revealed his inner thoughts. But, a pressing matter now weighed on him.

After having taken the group to the hospital in Puerto Ángeles, Nicolás began asking himself: why was the young gringo so interested in going out to the falls? While Jorge and Bill were still in town Nicolás´ curiosity had prompted him to make his own trip to the falls. He had cautiously walked amongst the trees, vines, and other vegetation, his hand all the while nervously rubbing the pistol that hung from his hip. No snake was going to take him by surprise.

"What could the *gringo* want out here? There must be something. After all, they had risked running into trouble. Just look at what happened to the boy. One thing I do know, if he came all the way to San Juan, and is so interested in this spot, there has to be some money in it somewhere." These thoughts had been gnawing at him ever since the group had taken their trip to the falls. Originally, Nicolás thought that the gringo was going to buy some land to start up a plantation. But, his opinion changed with his own investigation of what Bill was interested in. He saw the freshly cut vegetation and had reluctantly kicked around the plants with his boot, always watching for a snake. Then he saw it, the crevice in the rocks.

"A cave, a mine! That's what he was doing. He has found an old mine. I knew it! It's probably one the Spaniards worked years ago."

"I never heard of it from anybody, not even back in the company days. So, now I know our visitor's secret. He was probably going to buy the land cheap and put in a mining company." Nicolás stood pensively, considering the import of his discovery, and how he could profit by it.

These thoughts had been occupying his mind for the last few days. When Jorge and Reina had left the store he felt it was time to act, and now he knew the right way. Now, he had a plan of his own.

Chapter 12
The Unwilling Partner

J orge was conversing with Santiago about some work that needed to be done in the *Camote* patch. The two were surprised that Nicolás, unannounced and uninvited, suddenly appeared on his horse. The old man thought how nice it would have been had he gone to the patch himself and wasn't present to receive the visitor.

At the back of the house, leaning against a tree, Bill had much to think about and wasn't aware of the arrival of the horse and its rider. Nicolás, acting as if he owned the place opened up the side gate and walked in leading his horse. He tied up the reins on a post and then strode in the direction of Jorge.

"Well, *Don* Jorge, how is it going?"

"We are doing pretty good, thanks." Then with insight, knowing full well that Nicolás wasn't interested in any of them, he inquired of the reason for the unsolicited appearance.

"What brings you over to my house?"

"I want to speak with your young friend. Is he around?"

Then, as if fishing for information he said," Or, is he out riding? I heard he had been out by where your boy had been bit by the *Barba*. You probably left something out there when you left in such a hurry." He paused, giving Jorge a chance to provide him with any detail that could be helpful.

The old man managed to raise one corner of his mustache and grunt, but chose not to comment on the attempt to extract any probable cause for the ride to the falls.

"No, he isn't out riding around. He is here." Looking at Santiago he encouraged him to busy himself with some of his chores. The two men were left alone, and Jorge wasn't in a hurry to break the silence and initiate a conversation.

"Let me go call him for you." He went around the corner of the house and walked over to where Bill was standing. At seeing the old man he shook off his thoughts and stood erect.

"Nicolás is here and he wants to speak with you." The tone of his voice indicated that nothing good was to be expected.

"With me! What for?"

"You will have to ask him what he wants." The two walked unhurriedly.

Jorge paused a moment and looked at him. He locked his fingers on his forearm as someone wishing to protect a friend.

"Be careful." The warm paternal interest was obvious, and it didn't pass unnoticed by his young friend.

"Yeah, I know. He is up to something." They continued walking.

"*Señor* Walker, good to see you."

"How are you *Don* Nicolás?"

"Just fine. I know this is a surprise visit, but there was something that I wanted to talk over with you." His eyes settled on Jorge. "It would probably be better if we spoke in private." The old man understood what was inferred.

"I will leave you two alone to consider your business." He didn't like being told what to do in his own house, and especially by Nicolás. However, unlike his neighbor he believed in civility and so took his leave.

"So, what do you want to talk about with me?" He had come right to the point, and Nicolás wasn't quite ready to respond. Yet, this served as a prompt for him to do just that.

"Guillermo." He was trying to gain his confidence by addressing him in this manner. Pronouncing the name with a definite Spanish intonation.

"As you know, I am a business man. I have lived in this area for some time and I know many people, influential people. You know, people that can help out when you need to get things done." It sounded like he was trying to convince himself of his own importance.

"I would be a very helpful person to anyone who, let us say, wanted to do business in this country." Bill was lost in this web of desultory expressions that Nicolás was weaving. He wasn't sure where the conversation was going.

"Let me be open with you my young friend." The tone almost sounded condescending. "If you would like to mine gold or silver here, then I am the one you want to have on your side. You know, like a partner. You understand?"

"Mine gold or silver? Nicolás, what are you talking about? I am not planning on anything that has to do with a mine." He couldn't grasp the context of the words that he had just heard, but he could sense a malevolent intent.

"My young friend." That expression was beginning to annoy Bill. "I know about the cave. I was out there." This expression left his lips with a triumphant tone, but in subdued words. A vocal checkmate as he considered it.

Bill heard the word "cave" and his body suddenly tightened. He dissembled as best he could, his mind processing the words he had just heard. Did Nicolás know about the statue? His eyes scanned from side to side. How could he know about the statue? Was somebody watching out there?

"Go on, I am listening to you." He needed more information. What did Nicolás really know?

"You see, it is a very good thing to take me into your confidence." His sweaty hand grasped Bill's arm in a supposed expression of amiability. "Now, what is there? Gold? Silver?"

The foreigner's composed face belied the way his mind was racing through the details. The words echoed in his ears, "Gold, silver, a mine." The expressions indicated that Nicolás didn't know about the statue. He was thinking that some mineral deposit was to be exploited.

Bill said nothing while he mentally processed the situation and the need to lead him astray, or confuse him? After what seemed like an eternity to Nicolás, the foreigner spoke.

"Didn't you know anything about it?"

"No, no. I didn't know anything until, well, until I went out to the falls and found where you had been chopping around. You see it was rather curious how you were so interested in that area. Imagine, here is a mine under my own nose, and you have to come from so far to help me find it. Rather strange isn't it?" He laughed, which was an awkward camouflage for his obnoxious personality.

"What I meant to say is that you came from so far and found it. But, you will need a partner, someone who knows the right people, how things are done in this area. You know what I mean." Yes, he knew what he meant. People who could be bought to look the other way, to ignore facts, lie, cheat. His connotation of knowing the right people was understood clearly. Bill needed time to think. How was he going to keep Nicolas at bay and protect the statue?

"Let me think it over tonight. Tomorrow I will stop by your place and we can talk some more on how we can work together on this. Is that o. k.?" The amiability that radiated from Nicolás was sickening.

"Sure. Sure, no problem. Come by early, I will be waiting." His smile allowed the sun to glisten as it danced upon those two prominent gold teeth.

"You take care now my young friend and we will speak tomorrow. Oh, and one more item, it would be good to not talk with anyone else about this matter. You know how complicated all this could become if others found out." He paused, and then added. "Especially don't speak with Jorge. He is a simple man and doesn't understand business deals like this. I think it is best, don't you?" He didn't expect an answer, just an acknowledgement of the certainty of what he considered to be proper. Nicolás didn't need confirmation of anything that he felt to be true. Especially now, as his tactic had cornered the foreigner, or so he thought.

"Well, this has complicated things. At least I was able to throw him off the scent for a while. What do I do?" Bill watched him as he rode off on his horse

With his thoughts tumbling about he wasn't aware that Jorge had walked up behind him.

"So, he left, good." The undetected presence of the old man startled him.

"Yeah, he's gone." Jorge noticed the concerned worry in his voice. He waited what he considered to be an appropriate amount of time before asking.

"Did he say anything of importance?" The question was sincere and it met with a pained and perplexed expression.

"Can I help in some way, or is it a personal matter?" Bill pursed his lips, pushing his anxiety outward in a breath of air.

"Well, he knows about the cave where the statue was. But, he is not aware of what was in the cave. He thinks that a silver or gold mine is out there." Bill allowed himself a pathetic worried laugh. "Maybe emeralds waiting for him. I don't know exactly."

"You have trouble my young friend. Nicolás will not allow you to get your precious statue out of here. What is he asking from you?" There was a pause.

"He wants to be my partner." Jorge considered that statement and it obviously provoked some amusement in the old man.

"Allow me to be the first to congratulate you. You have a wonderful partner." The facetious comment didn't enliven his spirit. "Come on over here and sit down."

The two relocated to a shady area. Jorge sat in a hammock, Bill on a short three-legged stool. They sat in those positions for a few minutes, saying nothing, each trying to form their multiple thoughts into some cohesive plan of action. Bill then sat up straight, his face reflecting the arrival of a possible solution.

"*Don* Jorge. Why don't I let him have his gold mine?"

"Let him have it? What do you mean there isn't any gold out there."

"You know that, and I do as well. But, he doesn't. If I take him on as a partner, or let him think that he is, that will keep him busy while I get out of here somehow." Considering the option provided Jorge with a bit of levity as he imagined the chagrin that Nicolás would feel in being outwitted.

"He is a clever man." He reflected on his words. "No, he is a cunning man. I don't know how you can slip out without his taking notice of it. Do you think you can just get back to Puerto Ángeles and catch a plane, and then it is all over? No, you would have to think of something else."

While the two were wrestling with these thoughts, Nicolás and Inés in a rare moment of marital communication were analyzing the details from another perspective.

"How do you know that he has found something valuable? You think that with all of the men who have worked around here, the company with its plantations, that no one ever came across a mine? No it can't be anything other than just some hole in the ground." Her incredulity was irritating. He said nothing, shrugging his shoulders and denying his ears the right to hear any further words from that acerbic mouth.

He raised the coffee cup to his lips while his mind raced, pushed more rapidly by his tortured thoughts than by the caffeine. This chance of a lifetime was not to be missed. Still, the *gringo* could leave. But then, what of it? There would be more for him. He couldn't take the mine with him. What if he had some kind of legal paper or deed? Maybe he has already purchased the property and mining rights. His father was well known, and enjoyed the confidence and respect amongst the company heads. Could it be that he has friends in the capital that would help him? With such thoughts sprinting uncontrolled he became more agitated.

"Well, aren't you afraid that the *gringo* will outwit you somehow? You aren't listening to me Nicolás." Her voice went into shrill mode. "Nicolás!"

"Yes, yes I can hear you! Now, for once will you stop bothering me!" He rose suddenly from his chair. Her haranguing had reached the point where she knew it was time to back off. She could well remember the physical results when his anger came to the boiling point.

"I am going to Puerto Ángeles and I will be back tomorrow."

"To town? I thought you said you had to see the *gringo* tomorrow." His reply was decisive and given in a tone of warning.

"I said I am going into town." At this point she understood it was time to take her leave, he had come to the limit of his patience with her. She let out a billow of air and left for the front of the store where she dropped her weight on the counter supported by her elbows. Her hands cradling the plump round face with the bulging eyes staring in fixation out the window.

Nicolás gulped the last portion of his coffee and placed the cup unceremoniously on the table. Smoothing out his mustache with his fingers he turned his attention to his pants, jerking them up as high as the accumulation at his hips would allow. Then to obtain the items he needed he hurried from place to place in the house.

"Let me see, the keys are here in the basket. I will need some extra cash, three hundred should do." He counted it out delighting in the feel of the paper in his hands. As he maneuvered it into his front pocket his eyes fell upon the pistol in the steel box from which he had retrieved the money.

"I don't want to forget you." It was placed with some care between his ample stomach and his pants. Then he was out the door and soon the truck was on its way. Inés was still sulking.

"There he goes. Oh, that man irritates me to no end. Who knows what he really does in town?" It may have served to lessen her grief if she had known that he did have a valid reason for going, this time. He needed to check on who owned the land where the cave was located. Had Bill purchased it? Did he have some sort of legal rights over the land, or, was it national property? He also wanted to make a visit on an influential acquaintance, Colonel Guzmán.

Up the road from the store one of Jorge's children had come bouncing into the back yard. Bill and his host were still forging the details of their idea into some sort of general plan. As usual, the children of the village were informed of the comings and goings of their neighbors.

"Papá, Nicolás is going to Puerto Ángeles in his truck. Benito just told me that he will be gone all day and won't be back until tomorrow."

"That's nice daughter that you told me, now run along. Bill and I are talking." The young girl took her leave, bounding out with as much energy as she had entered. As he watched the disappearing form rounding the corner of the house he voiced his opinion on the report from his daughter.

"It would be nice if he just kept driving and didn't come back."

"What's that? I didn't quite hear what you said."

"I said it's a shame that he just doesn't keep driving and forgets to come back." They both gave thought to that idea.

"If you were to turn the statue over to the authorities would they give you something for it?" As he allowed his mind to dwell on that possibility he pulled a small pocketknife from his pants and began to whittle on a stick.

"Yeah, they would give me something." There was a note of negativity in his voice. "No one is to remove artifacts from the country without the permission of the authorities. That is the law and I know what will happen. If I abide by the law and turn the statue over, they say thank you and I will get my name in some paper, while someone else will get richer and that's it." He thought for a moment, and then his comments became almost sinister.

"Or, they may think there is a hoard of treasure somewhere and I am holding out on them. Then to help me tell them what they think I know, they arrange to extract the information from me in an unsavory manner, and then they make me disappear after not being able to tell them what they want. No, the best thing I can do is just to get out of here the fastest way possible." No one spoke, the silence punctuating the conversation.

"If you can help me find a way to get out, I am willing to pay you. In fact, with what I can obtain from the statue I could make your life better than you can imagine. Think about that! Your children would never have to face the privations of poverty." Jorge understood the implication of the comment, though the meaning of the word "privations" was unintelligible to him. In short order he replied to the offer.

"Have you ever seen the inside of one of our prisons here? I don't want to risk the happiness we already have. When I lay down at night, I don't worry about who is behind me, or who is at my door. I eat my food that I have grown. I share it when there is a good harvest. I am happy. And, I think my children will be happy too." There was little that could be said in reply to that comment, so the two sat in silence. Each of the men allowed the details to occupy their thinking. Having come to a conclusion Jorge finally spoke up.

"For the respect that I have for your father's memory I am going to help you get out. What you do after that is your business." Bill didn't know how he could do it, but, if anyone could it would be Jorge.

Chapter 13
Escape By Sea

J orge had a friend, a welder by the name of Francisco. This acquaintance had moved from the mainland to one of the two islands located 30 miles off of the coast. They were tropical in their flora and fauna and protected by reefs with clear azure waters. Their beaches, decorated by palms, made them a paradise setting. One was fairly large, almost 15 miles long and some 6 miles wide with a central mountain ridge running the length of the island. The other was smaller in landmass. These mountains projecting themselves from the sea, we're the scene of a lively fishing business, mainly for shrimp and lobsters.

There was a sizeable fleet of boats that called the islands their homeport. In fact, a fleet of shrimpers worked the area southeast of the islands where shallower waters and submerged reefs were to be found. On the main island a packing plant had been built. Shrimp and lobsters would be brought in and processed at the plant, then packaged and shipped abroad.

The boats served as a conduit for the bounty from the sea, taking their cargo to nearby ports. Finding their way into the holds of the ships, the lobsters, shrimp and fish were a reputable commodity. However, other cargo traveling clandestinely was also inserted amongst the boxes of frozen lobster and shrimp. The process would be reversed with merchandise working its way back to the islands. Some items were listed on the manifest, while others were quietly unloaded and received by smaller boats under the cloak of night.

In past centuries English pirates had originally settled the area. This biological and cultural inheritance had left a stamp on the facial features of the native islanders, and in the particularly dated English they chose as their everyday speech. Officially Spanish was the main language, and was spoken as the principle language by those who had come from the mainland. A paradox of the native islanders world was their aversion to anything Latin. They referred to the mainlanders as 'The Spanish', though they all shared the same nationality.

Francisco worked at the processing plant, and he was the one who Jorge and Bill had settled on to aid them in their plan. Jorge knew about the ships and their routes. He felt that if Bill was to get out with his statue it had to be on one of those ships. Francisco could be counted on to help, as he knew whom to approach on securing passage. This was the plan that had been decided on.

The two would leave in the early morning hours from San Juan and hopefully avoid calling attention to themselves. Just what the neighbors might consider as a fishing trip, plus a few details and comments that would indicate something else to those who heard of the outing. Supposedly, there was no reason for Nicolás to get wind of the excursion, though Jorge was counting on him hearing. With a little disinformation given to the right neighbors he might think they had gone to Puerto Ángeles, which was what Jorge really wanted him to think.

Arrangements were made for the boat trip to the island with one of his neighbors who owned a dory, a boat hallowed out of the trunk of a Ceiba tree. It had a small engine attached through a rather un-engineered opening to a propeller. They could leave early in the morning and make it to the main island while there was still daylight. That is if there were no mishaps.

Two years before a dory had gone into Puerto Ángeles with a collection of passengers. The owner was to pick up flour, as well as sugar along with other items that were needed in San Juan. As the dory came into the wharf it had struck one of the posts or pylons with excessive force. No one bothered to take note that on the bottom of the vessel, following the grain of the wood, a crack now ran down its length. On the way back in the heavy afternoon sea and with a full load of goods and people, the sudden dull cracking of the dory from one end to the other signaled the end of the voyage, as the boat split completely. In the panic everyone on board drowned, except the owner and his girlfriend who clung to a piece of the boat that remained on the surface. Some fishermen eventually found them.

Bill had never traveled in a dory before so this would be a first for him. Jorge had spoken with the owner of the dory and they were scheduled to leave at 4:00 am the next morning.

All was done rather hurriedly, they didn't have the luxury to wait and see how affairs would turn out with Nicolás. Jorge had wisely told the right people who could be counted on to inform every one that he and his visitor would be leaving in the dory. He left the destination said, and unsaid as he mentioned Puerto Ángeles, fishing up coast, down coast and several other probable locations.

It was early in the morning, after a rather sleepless night wrestling with the unknown that they left San Juan behind, heading towards the island, La Isla del Pino.

They had been gone a few hours when Nicolás returned. The noisy arrival of the truck provoked some unexpected excitement to start the day. He was radiant with the success of his trip. He had learned that the land belonged to the government. The fruit company had returned it to the public when its one hundred-year lease expired. And no one, not the foreigner, nor Jorge had initiated any purchase, lease or use of the area where the cave was. The visit to Colonel Guzmán had been just what had been expected, a brilliant tactic, or so Nicolás thought.

The Colonel, with the scent of money in the air had seen the advantage of becoming party to the matter, eliminating the *gringo* as soon as possible, and then helping exploit the riches.

Shutting the truck off and then swinging down from the cab Nicolás enjoyed a good stretch before strutting towards the house. His exploits had given him a tremendous appetite, and what a beautiful day it was, until he saw Inés. She was standing in the middle of the kitchen supervising some of the worker girls. Her hands were on her hips, head back, and her permanent scowl in place. His joy evaporated almost immediately upon seeing her.

The girls knew it would be best to busy themselves with their chores and leave the two to their petty squabbles. What entertainment it provided, and what delicious expressions passing between the two would the girls have to share with the neighbors.

"Do you have some coffee for me? I feel hungry, so get me some food."

This was a customary greeting and Inés wasn't prompted to a faster pace by it. Much different was the reaction of the girls who immediately obeyed the command of the master. A plate of beans, a little cheese, a scrambled egg and a stack of tortillas were soon on the table. His cup of coffee, steaming and filling the air with its sweet heavy smell was placed on the table as well. Before he sat down he took hold of a plastic glass. Dipping it into the opening of one of the clay pots in the kitchen he retrieved some water and rapidly emptied it. With one of his hands he wiped off the water that had settled on his mustache, and then fixed his eyes on his wife. A slight smile formed on his face that was extremely unsettling to Inés.

"The *gringo* hasn't come yet, eh?" One of the girls answered.

"No, *Don* Nicolás, nobody has come by this morning."

"Good. When he does come have him go outside and sit by the hammocks." As of yet Inés hadn't spoken a word, so it was time for some negative comment.

"You think he will be here this early? It will be an hour or more before he comes." She could always be counted on for a contrary view, a pessimistic observation, something to irritate him.

"Maybe so, maybe not, I will wait and see. I need to eat now anyway." With that said he sat down and rapidly the food disappeared from his plate accompanied with slurps and gulps.

He was nervous, apprehensive and in no mood for talking. Money was involved, and that was a theme that always quickened his pulse. In his mind he was exploring all of the ramifications of what might, or might not be said when he considered the need for Bill to politely exit this entire matter before something unpleasant were to occur. It was comforting for him to know that he had the authorities on his side. The Colonel could be counted on. How could a lone foreigner take on the commander of the battalion for this area? Others had tried, and they just suddenly disappeared.

With little ceremony he rose from the table, thanking no one. His leaving the kitchen was accompanied by his customary grunts belches and snorts, as well as the clearing of his throat. Once outside he turned his mind to washing the truck. Not that he would do it, rather, he told some of the young boys sitting on a nearby bench that he had some work for them if they wanted it.

As he organized the project he would periodically cast a glance looking for the expected visitor. As much as he hated to admit it, most likely his wife was right. It would be an hour or so. His suspicious nature began to flower and formed a host of worst-case scenarios. He would try to eliminate his concerns by reminding himself that the land hadn't been purchased, that he had the Colonel on his side. What could happen to deprive him of the prize? Finally, he could see that he would have to hurry this matter along. He told one of the boys to go to Jorge's and let the *gringo* know that he was waiting for him. The boy hurried off and shortly was back with his ill received report.

"Well, what did he say?"

"*Don* Jorge and his friend weren't there. *Doña* Reina said they had left early this morning." The boy was not prepared for the reaction.

"What? Left this morning? Well, where did they go? What did she say?"

"They left with *Don* Omar in his boat."

"She said that? Quick boy, did she say they left with Omar?" It was debatable who was feeling the greater emotion, the boy in his fear that Nicolás was about to strike him, or Nicolás himself.

"No. I mean yes." The scene was reminiscent more of an interrogation with an unwilling criminal rather than an adult speaking with a young boy.

"Well, when I spoke with *Doña* Reina she said that her husband wasn't there. He and his friend had left with *Don* Omar and they were leaving in his boat." The boy was shaking and had turned rather pale. The words obviously had a difficult time in coming forth from his mouth.

"Why those miserable-." There was an emphatic gesture as he struck the flat of his right hand against the truck.

A cloud of dust rose as he kicked the ground, an outlet for his emotions. The actions were more those of a petulant child than an adult. But, what was to be expected from Nicolás? The boy though was relieved to see that it was the truck and the ground that were the victims of the outburst, and not his small frame.

"They have gone. But, where did they go?" He muttered his thoughts aloud. The boy ventured to answer hoping to gain some approval.

"I heard from my friend Tomás that they went to Puerto Ángeles." Jorge was right, the right people had been told the wrong information.

"Puerto Ángeles?" What are they doing there? The *gringo* knew he had to be here this morning. Why did they go with Omar in his boat? If they needed to go to town couldn't they have waited for the train, or ask me to take them? They are up to something." He began to pace, his hands resting on his waist, the thoughts whirring about, bouncing off of each other.

"No, they didn't ask me, and they didn't wait because they want to cut me out. They have some idea on how to get around me, deny me my opportunity." He was mumbling all of this to himself, but with sufficient volume so that the boys could hear him. A sudden halt to this bewildering monologue, and his shifting his attention to them prompted their immediate busying of themselves with the rags in their hands. It would be to their benefit to continue polishing what they could on the truck and distance themselves as best they may.

"All right. So they have some idea of their own. Well, we will see who wins."

The tempest brewing in San Juan wasn't noticed by Jorge and Bill who were now some miles from the mainland. As far as the weather was to be considered, it was a perfect day. The sea was calm with a light breeze. The swells gently rolling under the bow of the boat lifting it, and allowing it to gently settle back before another would raise it anew.

The dory had no keel and was completely rounded underneath. It had been fashioned by hallowing out the trunk from a suitable tree for the size of the boat desired. With no keel it wasn't unusual for it to roll over if the swells were not entered with precaution, dumping the passengers and cargo into the sea. Water invariably would accumulate inside from cracks or openings, or at times a swell managed to creep over the boat's edge. The owner would appoint someone to use a plastic bowl and continually bail out the accumulating seawater. It was powered by a large lawn mower engine modified somewhat and appropriately geared in such a way as to power a shaft which projected from the rear of the boat. Connected to the shaft was a propeller, likewise a homemade arrangement of dubious reliability, but it was functional. Such mechanical marvels were considered by the locals as a good means of travel to reach the islands.

Omar thought it rather curious that Jorge and his friend wished to spend an entire day traveling to the Isla del Pino, which was their destination. Maybe for Jorge it wasn't out of character, even though he wasn't accustomed to trips to the island, but traveling in the dory wouldn't be strange for him as a local man. However, why would the *gringo* travel in a dory when he could go back to Puerto Ángeles and catch a plane? It would have been quicker. Jorge hadn't mentioned the reason for the trip, and Omar wasn't asking. The old man's money was just as good as the next man's.

Bill was glad to have his hat as the day began to warm and provided him with some shade, and there was no shade in the boat. He sat in the front looking out over the bow. Jorge was in the middle and Omar in the back where he could regulate the engine, as well as steer the boat with the rudder.

"Bill! Hey, Bill!" He turned around as best he could to see what Jorge wanted. Doing so with a good deal of caution, staying centered in the vessel so as not to provoke a roll over.

"Yeah. What do you want?"

"What do you think of the trip?" Jorge had slipped into a happy mood with the invigorating smell from the sea and the novelty of the voyage.

"It is beautiful out here. The boat runs pretty good as well." He stayed partially turned for a moment. "How far out do people go in these things?"

"At times they go way out to fish. Sometimes so far out that you can't see land." That prompted Bill to turn with a noticeable jerk of his head.

"Not see land? No thanks, that's not for me. Too far." Omar, who was listening to the conversation, was amused by the comment. For years he had been in and out of boats, in good weather, and bad. He had transported merchandise, passengers, occasionally going north to the reefs to bring back whatever he could catch in the way of fish. For him the sea was his backyard so he added his comments in its defense.

"Take it from me *Don* Guillermo, you would love it. So peaceful, just you and the sea."

"Yeah, too much sea that's the problem." Omar now felt relaxed enough with his passengers to rummage around in a sack he had brought along. In short order he pulled out a bottle of *Aguardiente* and enjoyed a rather large serving. He grimaced somewhat, but with a note of pleasure. After this encounter with his acquaintance of many years his eyes reddened, he cleared his throat, but avoided spitting so as not to lose any of the precious liquid that remained in his mouth. He let out a bellow that startled his two passengers. Turning their heads they saw him cork his bottle and realized the reason for his sudden shout of exuberance.

Bill facing straight in front was allowing the breeze to rush over his face. He studied how the prow plied through the swells effortlessly, rising and falling rhythmically. Around him was the immensity of the sea, the light reflected and danced on its surface. This was the same sea where *La Doncella* had once sailed. He looked down, pushing softly with his foot against his backpack, reassuring himself that it was still there.

Chapter 14
The Colonel

Inés continued to mull over her husband's actions. She knew enough to stay out of his way and so resigned herself to watch him from the kitchen window. He was resting one hand on a palm tree and rubbing his stomach with the other, which action was prompted by the inconformity of his digestive track with the present situation.

The worker girls were busy washing out clothes using a scrubbing board and a large yellow bar of soap. They carried out their task with such vigor that the buttons were frequently ripped from the garment. However, they were not so busy that they couldn't raise their eyes over the shirts, or the other garments from time to time and glance in the direction of Nicolás who obviously was giving much thought to something.

Soon enough, his sulking meditation passed. He stood erect as if called to attention. Grabbing both sides of his belt and pants he pulled them up and made a failed attempt to encompass his stomach. Then, he cleared his throat with horrid grunts of frustration mixed with indignation.

"All right, they want to cut me out. Well, let's see who is the smartest."

Casting that declaration into the air he headed for his truck. His hands were shaking at this point, but he managed to fumble about in his pockets looking for his keys. When once they had been found he pulled himself up into the seat and quickly brought the truck to life, alerting the dogs that it was time to raise their heads and prepare themselves for the chase.

His wife had taken up some work in the kitchen, a rare event. She usually enjoyed supervising the girls, complaining and offering unsolicited and unnecessary comments on how something should or should not be done. Now however, she was frying some plantains in camouflaged indifference to her husband's actions. The noise of the truck's engine called her to the window again. She watched, wondering why he was not parking it in the accustomed spot. Her curiosity got the better of her and she started for the door at the back of the house. Diesel fumes could be smelt in the air. He was obviously irritated and in a hurry. Soon a shout was trumpeted from the house.

"Why aren't you going to park it under the trees?" No reply was given. She moved to a closer position. "Hey, where are you going to leave it?" The brief reply was given in a gruff bawl.

"I'll be back tomorrow."

"Tomorrow? Where are you going you just got here this morning?" No reply was given.

This sudden activity was just too much for her. She had nothing to say. Standing there with her hands on her hips she watched the truck bed twist momentarily as it adjusted to the slope of the terrain. And then, it was gone.

The girls had stopped washing. They were looking at their mistress who stood with her mouth partially opened gazing in disbelief at what had transpired. Her husband to be sure was a rare individual. But this behavior, what could account for it? She looked around to see if one of the neighbors was near. Possibly someone had given Nicolás an urgent message, or something had happened. No one was there. With heavy, indecisive steps, she walked slowly to the edge of the road. Could it be that he had stopped at one of the neighbors? No, the truck had headed towards the main road, and was on it's way to Puerto Ángeles.

Nicolás had studied his options and felt that he knew the best course to take. He was going to solicit the help of someone in authority; someone who could thwart the plans that he felt somehow had been made to circumvent him. Jorge and his friend were seeking to deny him the money that must be involved. He was certain that the foreigner had come upon a gold or silver mine. How he knew it was there was irrelevant at this point. What needed to be done was to get it away from him.

His distracted frame of mind made for some erratic driving. The truck would speed up, then slow down, make an overreaction to a pothole looming up ahead, swerving to miss it, then coming back to a straight course. The entire trip was carried out in the same fashion. Irrespective of his speed, it was taking too much time for him. He passed people sitting on the side of the road. Individuals who were watching over collections of oranges, bananas and assorted clay pots they had made. All of these goods were on their way to town. No consideration was shown as he passed them. The truck threw dust into the air, scattering the hopeful vendors back into the undergrowth of bushes and trees. The dust eventually settled, lightly coating everything, even the leaves of the undergrowth that took on a pale aspect.

His plan required contacting Colonel Guzmán, and letting him know what the foreigner and Jorge were obviously up to. The Colonel was the military head of the local battalion, and as such, he did what he personally delighted in for his own amusement or benefit. He would be the one to put a stop to this plan of the *gringo* and his host. After all, the Colonel was a friend, or so Nicolás thought.

The truck and its driver eventually survived the road and approached the town. He crossed over the bridge at the outskirts of Puerto Ángeles, scarcely taking notice of the women washing clothes, several taxi drivers with their cars, and of course, the never ending crop of children. All of these had congregated at the river, to wash, polish, play, benefitting by the ready source of water, which as of yet no one had begun to charge for.

Choosing his route, the most direct, he navigated along the streets to the battalion headquarters, or *La Base*. A combination of mesh wire fencing and an old adobe wall surrounded it. At the main entrance two soldiers stood, or better said, slouched in a rather careless position of indifference, leaning against a sentry post booth. However, upon seeing the truck they snapped into a picture of military preparedness. The camouflaged uniforms, steel helmets, a vest supposedly impervious to bullets, and the rifles they held all spoke of authority, not so much of practicality as the heat was stifling. The truck came to a stop at the checkpoint. The soldiers took up positions on opposite sides of the vehicle, studying cautiously what this invader was. With utmost brevity and an air of self-importance the sentry on the driver's side spoke up.

"Your business here, Sir."

"I wish to speak with Colonel Guzmán."

"Your name?" The terse manner of address was rather unnerving for Nicolás. He didn't appreciate being spoken to in such a manner.

"Your name, Sir?" The second command finally coerced him into divulging the information being requested. Clearing his throat he croaked.

"Nicolás Leva."

"Wait here." The soldier walked towards the booth where he picked up a phone, all the while studying the intruder with a careful eye.

On the other side of the truck stood his companion, who nervously ran his finger around the guard on the rifles trigger, saying nothing but with a look of malevolent intent on his face. He had been taught well to project the austere and machinelike coldness expected of him. In reality, he was a conscript, a mere boy who had been forcibly recruited.

In seeking new recruits a rather novel form of the draft was invented. A military vehicle would pull up in front of a theater and wait until the movie was over. When the crowd came out soldiers would begin grabbing young men of an appropriate age, dragging them towards the truck and throwing them into the back where they were persuaded to stay by two soldiers with their weapons held in a ready position. They were then driven to the local barracks and dressed in an appropriate ill-fitting uniform. Their heads were shaved, eliminating any chance of an infection of lice, and then appropriately instructed by means of shouts, insults and occasional blows that they were now soldiers, rendering a sacred duty to the homeland. There was not much patriotism involved in this manner of recruitment, but it did supply the bodies needed.

It was another oppressively hot day, or so it seemed to Nicolás who was sweating copiously, most likely more from anxiety than the heat. The soldier emerged from the booth after finishing the phone call informing his superior that a request had been made for an interview with the Colonel. Authoritatively, he instructed Nicolás that he could enter, where he was to park the truck, and how a soldier awaiting him in the parking area would accompany him to the office.

Easily enough he found the parking area where he saw the soldier waiting for him. Climbing out of the vehicle with some difficulty, as his legs had stiffened during the drive, he greeted the soldier. This one displayed more civility than the sentries, even exchanging a few pleasantries with Nicolás. Obviously, he was a professional. Men of his sort usually languished in levels of rank that did not pose a threat to superiors engaged in profitable, though unethical actions.

Nicolás was taken to the administrative center of the base, a rather unimpressive sterile looking building. Over the door hung a sign; *"COMANDANCIA GENERAL."*

He cleared his throat. The escort instructed him to open the screen door and enter. A soft breeze from ceiling fans kept the flies disoriented and apparently incapable of landing on those inside. A young soldier looked up at him from his desk.

"*Señor* Leva. You are here to see the Colonel I understand. I will tell him you have arrived." He rose, walked over to a door leading into the office where the Colonel was to be found and knocked lightly. The resonant, raspy voice of a man obviously a smoker answered.

"Yes." The soldier opened the door.

"Sir. *Señor* Leva has arrived. Does the Colonel wish me to show him in?" A creaking office chair indicated that the Colonel was positioning himself to receive the visitor.

"Yes, have him come in."

"Very good, Sir." The soldier turned towards Nicolás, stepping to one side and holding the door open with an extended arm.

"*Señor* Leva, you may go in." With access now granted Nicolás prepared himself. His mouth seemed rather dry, his lips stiff. The right hand was busy smoothing down his mustache. Clearing his throat again he managed a cordial thanks to the soldier and walked into the office. The door was immediately closed behind him.

The Colonel was wearing a baggy camouflaged uniform, which obviously suited well the rather portly figure not easily hidden behind the desk. His name, written in large black letters, was clearly visible on his chest, just above pocket level. He would rather wear his dress uniform with the awards, citations, medals and other indications of his worth. They had been awarded more for his complicity in questionable conduct with his superiors and keeping his mouth shut, than for any meritorious military action. But, today he was wearing the loose fitting camouflaged uniform that was certainly more comfortable for day-to-day affairs.

"Nicolás, what brings you here?" He could see that his guest was nervous, which the Colonel enjoyed. He was enamored of his rank and enjoyed seeing people fawn over him, or grovel before his authority.

"It has to do with that mine I told you about. The *gringo* and the old man are up to something." The comment made the Colonel's face tighten, his lips protruding even more. Nicolás had initially brought him into his confidence when he last came to town. At that time he was seeking out information on the owner of the property, or if any claims had been filed on exploiting the wealth he knew must be involved.

"So, what are they doing?"

"They left San Juan this morning heading for here." He considered the comment and then glanced at the clock hanging on the wall.

"So, why have they come to town?"

"That is what I don't know. I am sure the old *campesino* and his friend are trying to get around us somehow." He felt it best to make mention of their 'getting around us', plural. The Colonel needed to realize that he could be a looser as well on this matter.

"Do you have any idea of where they are, or who they came to see?"

"No. I don't know what they are doing." His anxiety was obvious, squirming about in his chair as he was, fingering the hat held in his hands. The Colonel acknowledged all of this with a guttural grunt, considering the scanty details. He wasn't desirous of letting money slip by either, and Nicolás had convinced him that money was involved.

"We need to find out where they are in town first, and then who they are going to see." The comments were of such consolation to Nicolás that he began to feel at ease.

The two sat in silence until a torrent of questions, comments and thoughts passed between them. This went on for about 40 minutes as they tossed about options, finally arriving at a plan of action, which the Colonel was pleased to see as his own.

The plotting based on false premises went unnoticed by the three men who were well out to sea, and who would arrive at the island before the day was gone.

Chapter 15
The Island Of El Pino

T he dory was traveling at a good pace with the favorable weather and minimal resistance from the currents. In the distance the island of El Pino grew larger on the horizon. It and its sister island, that lay a few miles to the east, projected themselves upward from the ocean floor being the highest points of an undersea mountain chain.

The two islands rose from waters so transparent that the dories, which were anchored in the inlets or tied to the wharves, seemed to float in the air. Reefs protected the islands, allowing approach to them only through specific channels.

About an eighth of a mile from El Pino, the system of reefs came together to form an area raised above the reach of the waves. It was basically an incipient island with some mangrove swamps or sea grass surrounding a flat, dry solid interior. A bustling community dedicated to making a living from the sea was established on the dry ground.

Fishing was the main source of income for many, while others chose trades untrammeled by conscience. Wooden homes, shops and assorted structures clung tenaciously to this cay as it was called.

The population grew; the homes expanded outwards and eventually outgrew the scaffolding of dry earth. This was not seen as a deterrent. Homes were then built on pylons that had been driven down into the coral of the shallower depths. Wooden causeways on the periphery substituted for sidewalks and connected the dwellings in what was a somewhat bewildering pattern. Underneath these paths of local life the sea would pass unhindered by the invasion of people inhabiting this tropical Venice. On the outer edge of the settlement, where the sea was unchallenged, large schools of fish swam amongst the piers. The population continued to grow until the cay became a thriving communal cluster. Contributing to the growth was the presence of a local industry, a shrimp and lobster packing business that provided employment at a wage that allowed life to continue. This settlement was the destination of the three men in the dory.

The peaceful hours of sitting in the dory on the way to the island were soon to end. Omar was navigating around coral reefs, approaching from one of the access points. The engine was throttled down and the dory began to sink lower in the water, though still high enough to pass over the ascending sea floor, which was changing rapidly. The water took on a chameleon character as it altered from deep blue, to green, to turquoise. The depths giving way to the system of reefs, at times only a few feet below the bottom of the vessel. The clarity allowed glimpses of creatures and plants that thrived in the warmth and abundance of the shallows.

There was a noticeable difference between this friendlier haven within the reef and the undulating movement of the swells in the open sea. The masses of coral served as a protective wall not permitting the waves to pass beyond this outer frontier of the island.

Jorge and Omar were busy exchanging observations and each pointing to where they thought it best to tie up to the dock. When once it had been decided the dory was directed towards the destination and Omar readied his oar so he could negotiate the approach, maneuvering the vessel to where the journey ended.

"Let's get out." Those were refreshing words to all. Each one carefully positioned his legs beneath himself while trying to steady their hands on the wharf so as not to roll the dory too much to one side.

"Oh man, that feels good." Jorge shook his head in agreement with his friend's observation. He rubbed his legs with both hands coaxing life back into them.

"This body is getting old. Too old for these kinds of trips." Amongst grunts and yawns, stretches and other movements to resurrect their limbs, laughs and smiles were intermingled. All were thankful that they had arrived safely. Placing his hands on his back, and bending as far as his body would allow him in a gratifying stretch he cast a look in Omar's direction.

"Where do you plan on staying?" He didn't answer immediately but was occupied doing something to the motor. His laugh and the look of expectant deviant behavior on his face said much of what he was thinking. He finished his task and stood erect again. Wiping his hands on a rag that dangled from the front pocket of his trousers he replied to the inquiry.

"Oh, I'll find someplace. I have some friends here." He did have acquaintances as this was not his first trip to the island, and those friends usually didn't bring out the best in him.

Jorge had told him that they would be staying with Francisco, for what reason wasn't stated, nor did Omar really care. What was of importance to him was to be on his way, and to employ his energy in dissipation as soon as possible.

Bill was shouldering his backpack when he noticed two security force members looking over at the three recent arrivals. They were soldiers, as the security force was under the control of the military just as all of the government agencies were. The camouflaged uniforms, the rifles held carelessly, the burgundy colored berets nothing of what he saw inspired him with a sense of security. Outwardly he adopted an attitude of apathetic indifference, though his true feelings were far from unconcerned.

Omar and Jorge were seemingly unaware and unperturbed with the presence of the soldiers. They were involved in a discussion of when they would go back to San Juan, and if Omar needed the money for the passage now or later, which led to quite a discussion. The two had known each other for many years. There existed an amicable trust as was common amongst friends in San Juan.

Omar was weighing the facts, giving consideration to how much he thought he might spend and whether he would spend all he had, or lose it if it were given to him. The old man finally helped him decide by reminding him that money invited the company of others who would help spend it. So, they came to the common accord that Jorge would provide him with half of the price for the passage. This amount would be enough to punish his body worthily in wanton conduct, but allowing him some funds to take back home.

With the details attended to it was time for each to continue on their way, which Omar was grateful for. He was anxious to take up his diversion as soon as possible.

There were some handshakes and slaps on the back and they parted company wishing each other well.

As Omar disappeared around a corner Jorge directed himself to his visitor.

"Well, let's go see if we can find Francisco." With that statement made the two started heading to the other side of the cay.

Absorbed as they were with their reasons for having made the trip, they didn't give thought to how their appearance was somewhat out of character for the island. With little difficulty the locals identified them as being from the mainland due to their way of dress, the way of walking, and the most obvious, a *gringo* with an old *campesino*.

The curious gazes of the locals didn't stop the two from seeking out Francisco's house. They negotiated their way off of the wharf and onto some of the wooden causeways connecting the settlement, which to Bill's surprise were really quite sturdy. There were some areas where the planking was separated by an inch or so, and the water beneath and to the sides reminded them that taking a misstep and they would find themselves swimming.

The layout of the houses and assorted buildings didn't seem to follow any real pattern. At the center of the settlement there was solid ground that permitted some of the buildings to be made of blocks and cement. Ones like the bank, some public buildings for the government representatives, a few stores and then there were the homes of those who obviously controlled commerce on the islands.

One pleasantly situated was that of the Sergeant, who was the military official in charge. Like the rest of the residents he felt that there were less mosquitoes and it was cooler living on the cay away from the island proper of El Pino.

The packing plant took up the Northern side of the cay. There, shrimp and lobsters were unloaded from the boats and processed for shipment to foreign markets. A disproportional amount of *cantinas* and other enterprises that entertained the populace were also present. From this central area the buildings radiated out until the coral cay ended and the sea began. The causeways and suspended constructions started where the land ended. Everywhere was the smell of the sea carried by the breeze, except where the fetid odor of raw sewage was mixed with salt water.

The foundation below this social structure was the sea and what it produced, or what could be transported over it. Crews would ship out on the shrimp boats for months, and when the catch was plentiful they returned with their pockets full. Life on the cay was not the incubator of saints. Though there were those who kept themselves unspotted by avoiding dissolute wanderings. The majority lived for money, and they showed no compunction and saved no labor in obtaining it.

Amongst the population were those who presented themselves as being benign business people. They also were the pillars of the largest Protestant church on the island. This moral mask hid the paucity of ethics underneath, as they were the ones who controlled the contraband trade, which was a thriving enterprise, often turning violent.

Jorge and Bill had not eaten much on the way over. The distraction, nervousness and the movement of the sea had kept their appetites at bay. Now that they were employing their legs again and walking on firm ground, they became aware of the need for something to eat. More importantly, something to drink as the sun had coaxed a good deal of moisture from their bodies in the form of sweat.

As they passed by a small business Bill noticed that they had Tamarind water for sale. He pointed it out to his companion, who was of the same mind on the need for something. Yes, a glass or two might be called for, and soon enough they had purchased a mixture of the drink.

Bill held his glass up to the sun peering closely at the cloud of brown pulp swirling in the water. Who knows what parasites hid in the thick mixture? Jorge was watching him over the top of his glass. He knew what his visitor was thinking.

"Go ahead. It is rainwater. All the water here on the islands is rainwater. They store it in their cisterns. The rain is the only source of fresh water. Everybody else drinks it." With that culinary counsel taken into account he shrugged his shoulders in defeat to his thirst and drank it. It didn't have a bad taste, a little too sweet and it contained some of the strands from the Tamarind pods. But, it accomplished its purpose.

Jorge was arranging his mouth after the slightly acidic and overly sweet drink by moving his lips and tongue in such a manner as to clear the remnants of the Tamarind strands from his teeth. Looking at the lady he asked some information from her.

"Tell me, do you know Francisco Camacho? He works for the packing plant. Or, that is he used to, I don't know if he still does." She stopped stirring the large glass container that held one of her drinks. Studying for a moment the two men, she felt that they posed no threat and so spoke up.

"Yes, I know him."

"Does he still live at the far side of the cay at the end of the walkway?"

"Yes, he is still there. He wouldn't be at home now, not until after work, in about another hour or so, I think. Sometimes the plant works late. Depending on what takes place during the day. You are from the mainland aren't you?"

"Yes, we came over from San Juan today."

"San Juan! I have a sister who lives in San Juan." The conversation took on a friendly nature.

"Who is your sister?"

"Amilca Fernández."

"Amilquita? I know her well she is married to Gustavo. They have the plot of coconut palms on the edge of the village." She was obviously pleased that he knew her sister and was aware of their selling coconuts.

"And who are you?"

"Jorge Valladares." Remembering that he was not alone he pointed to Bill.

"And this is Guillermo Walker. He is visiting with me. His dad and I used to work for the company years ago." Her body language indicated she was pleased to meet both of them. Her eyes though displayed a marked preference for Bill, as he was not an everyday sight.

"Well, it's good to meet both of you. How long are you going to stay?"

"Not long, we are just visiting some friends like Francisco." She knew enough about life on the cay to not ask further questions on the reason for the visit. Sometimes it was best to not know too many details about what business people were involved in. Their exchange of pleasantries came to its end, the drinks were paid for, and they parted company with the two continuing their walk to the far side of the key.

Jorge realized that Francisco would still be at work, but considering the hour it wouldn't be long before he came home. So, their gait was unhurried, yet purposeful.

He was familiar with the way to the house. Though he hadn't been to the island for about three years, but not much of the basic layout of the walkways had changed. The area of solid ground limited more substantial building projects, as construction was limited on the periphery of the cay by the depth of the water. The settlement could only go so far until further growth became impractical, impossible. The two had advanced to where the island disappeared and beneath them was the sea. From this point on the construction of houses, buildings and walkways was held above the water by posts and pillars driven into the reef. This continued until the sea no longer permitted setting down posts for foundations, and then the settlement stopped.

As they negotiated the walkways, some well made and solid, but others obviously in need of repairs, they encountered the imposing presence of a woman. She had managed to force her voluminous body into a pleated, frilly white dress reaching down to her feet. The manner of dress seemed out of place to Bill. Her garment was made of light material to be sure, but to his way of thinking the heat and humidity didn't call for such sartorial elegance. He was unaware that this was the dress code for women of her social standing. She was the foremost member of the church choir, and her station called for impressing others with her appearance of piety.

The superior morality was only superficial, seeing that her family was the principal group of the contraband activity, and not adverse to unscrupulous or violent actions if their interests were threatened. As they passed each other, placing their feet carefully so as not to chance a fall into the sea, the three acknowledged the others presence with a nod of the head and a polite greeting.

Not far from the encounter with the choir lady a whirring noise caught Bill's attention. It was coming from a house. Like many of the simpler homes it had windows, but no glass, just wooden shutters. From one of these a red curtain had escaped the confines of the structure. It had draped itself outside and was gently moving in the wind. The shutters would be opened in the morning and closed at night for a measure of privacy. This construction was cheaper and far more practical as it allowed the sea breeze to lessen the heat of the day. It also provided an unencumbered means to speak with the neighbors, who if they chanced to pass by could easily see who was at home. No glass made for a perfectly fine way to keep tabs on everyone, assuring all that nothing was being missed. If a few minutes of gossip, or conversing about nothing of much importance was desired, it could be done by raising the voice a little as you spoke from the walkway with those inside, thus assuring that all the neighbors close by could hear. Hopefully this would initiate a general conversation amongst many who would stick their heads out their windows, or come outside to join in. On a small island any news or novelty is much appreciated.

Accompanying the whirring was the music from a radio, not an expensive one judging by the poor quality of the sound. The source of the activity was a home as well as a business. The owner had set up his tailor shop in the front room of his three room wood dwelling. There were six sewing machines each operated by its own pedal system. These machines were the source of the whirring noise, the man at each one pedaling to power his individual machine. The house, like all the construction in this part of the settlement was suspended over the water on posts, and at times the pedaling would synchronize to start a slight, but perceptible movement of the walkway.

Bill's steps slowed somewhat so he could study the view before him. One of the men looked up from his machine and saw the two. Bill smiled and waved, which gesture was reciprocated with an acknowledgment of a nod of the head, the tailor's hands were busy moving, folding, and sewing the material. This day they were finishing a lot of 50 pairs of pants destined to be sent on the next boat north, where hopefully they would soon be sold.

A younger brother of the owner of this business had grown restless with the confining environment of the island, and desirous of fulfilling his dreams he had moved abroad. After a few years of hard work he succeeded in starting up a small store, nothing to brag about, but it was his, and the older brother never tired of making mention of how he would send clothes to be sold in his brother's store.

As they approached the end of the walkway Francisco's house came into view. It was a modest wood dwelling, but with the appearance of being rather solidly built, the posts on which it sat being substantial and firmly anchored in the reef below. The walkway widened out becoming a platform patio allowing access to the door and the front windows. Jorge's pace picked up enlivened by knowing that they had almost arrived. Switching his bag from one shoulder to the other he leaned in the window and called out.

"Well, where are the good people who live here?" A few seconds passed before his next summons to the door. "Francisco, Teresa! There are two more for supper. Have we come in time?"

In the kitchen, which was not visible from the window, there was the movement of some pots and then a woman's voice cried out.

"I will be right there." Soon enough there was the movement of feet and a rather thin, but attractive women with her hair tied in a braid behind her head appeared from the kitchen. She was busy wiping her hands on a towel as she came into view by the visitors.

"Yes, can I help you?"

"We were told that the best food on the island is to be found in this home." Her steps slowed somewhat at this unusual statement. Then her face brightened as she recognized who had spoken.

"*Don* Jorge, what a surprise. What brings you to the island?" Her pleasure at seeing the friend from the mainland was obvious, producing a torrent of gestures and statements openly displaying her joy.

"Don't stand out there. Come in! Come in! Francisco will be so pleased to see you. Tell me, Reina and the children how are they? Are you by yourself?" Her eyes glanced in Bill's direction.

"Well, no. This fellow started following me when he heard that I was going to visit the best cook on the cay." The compliment was gratefully received with a polite laugh and an appropriate amount of diffidence.

"Jorge, you haven't changed at all. I am far from that."

"Teresa, this is a very good friend who is visiting from the States, his name is Guillermo. His father and I used to work together many years ago with the company." The syllables of 'many' were long and drawn out, as the details seemed distant, but the pleasure of youthful memories still persisted.

"Very nice to meet you. If you are a friend of this gentleman you are our friend too." Her words unpolished and lacking eloquence we're wrapped in sincerity and expressed from within.

"Please, don't stand here at the window. Come in! Francisco will soon be home." She rapidly moved to the door opening it wide and motioning animatedly with her hand to step in.

The house was modest, functional, but more importantly it was a home. The exterior somewhat painted, consisted of smooth surfaced wood planks fitting tightly one to the other. This siding was the only item separating the outside world from the activity within, as there were no interior walls, that is nothing to hide the wooden frame consisting of studs and beams, neither was there a ceiling. The roof over their heads was made of sheets of corrugated zinc securely fastened by screws to the rafters. A solid shell was formed protecting the family from the sun and rain. Inside all of the wood was painted a sky blue color. Unpretentious, that is what described the home, yet it had an air of tranquility, a place you would wish to come to at the end of the day.

Seeing that it was the last dwelling on the edge of the island there was nothing to block the wind. A breeze was traveling over the surface of the sea and it entered through the open windows, collecting the smell of the fish waiting in the kitchen and the recently diced onions. The open window in the back of the house framed the blue waters. Bill could see in the distance the mainland, its mountains resting on the swells.

Teresa's exuberance in having visitors made for no lack of conversation. She plied Jorge with questions on the family and details of daily life at home, his wife, the children, how the crops were doing. He managed to make short comments before a new question would send the conversation in another direction.

"Tell me Teresa, does Francisco still work at the packing plant?"

"Oh yes, he loves his job. There is always some machine that needs repairs, or welding to be done on the shrimp boats." She glanced at a table clock, one made in China with large numbers and two bells mounted on top for the alarm. "Francisco should be home any minute now. And, I can speak for him you are welcome to spend the night. We can set up two beds for you right here in the front room. No excuses either, you will eat with us."

"Well, why do you think we came out here? I have been bragging about your cooking." Then pointing to Bill he added. "This fellow wouldn't believe me unless I actually let him come and taste it for himself."

"Oh, Jorge." Her face flushed somewhat. As she realized how much she enjoyed the compliment.

Presented now with a challenge to live up to the praise her cooking was receiving, she excused herself. However, not before assuring the two guests that they were more than welcome to feel as if the home were their own.

At intervals the sound of a knife chopping, and of fish being lowered into hot grease was punctuated by the appearance of her head around the corner of the kitchen. She wished to continue her part in the conversation with the two guests. This animated exchange of comments continued on until the sound of approaching steps announced the arrival of her husband.

When Francisco opened the door his abrupt halt was noticeable. His eyes focused on the two men sitting in his house. He straightened up, instinctively standing tall not knowing what to expect.

"Well, I thought we would have to eat all of the food ourselves. But, I see you have decided to come home." Though said playfully, the somewhat gruff voice of the old man prompted an immediate reaction of seriousness. Soon enough relief and joy spread out over Francisco's face.

"Jorge! Well, what boat brought this old man out here?" Suddenly the house became the scene of handshakes and hugs intermingled with boisterous laughing and spontaneous comments. There was the customary exchange of formalities with each one informing himself of the others welfare, activities and state of health. Jorge introduced his companion, whom Francisco had been studying with a mixture of curiosity and anxiety.

"So, what pried you off of your *Camote* patch and brought you to my house?" With a measure of seriousness and presented in rather subdued tones Jorge replied.

"I have a matter that I need your help on."

"You need my help?" Francisco was incredulous. He always knew Jorge to be a self- reliant man, not wishing to inconvenience anyone by asking for help.

"What can I help you with?" Before Jorge could answer Teresa called out to say that supper was ready, and informed her husband that he needed to wash up and not detain his guests any longer.

"I can tell you after we eat."

As they took their places around the table, sitting on the two benches on either side, they studied the food that had been placed before them. Barracuda, fried in coconut oil was the main dish. Fried potatoes accompanied it, some chopped cabbage and a jar of vinegar sauce with spices and whole chilies were the garnish. Teresa had worked hard, and the flavor of fresh ingredients skillfully combined and prepared made for a delicious meal.

Francisco stopped everyone momentarily and announced that something was missing. Excusing himself he disappeared out the front door. Teresa seemed to know where he had gone and so she prompted the two guests to continue filling their plates. Within minutes he returned with three bottles of beer.

"Here, this will help out if you swallow a fish bone." He opened the bottles and sat them before his guests, with one for himself. Teresa didn't mind not having one; she never acquired a taste for beer.

"Teresa, this fish is so good I will eat the bones." Jorge didn't have to worry about the bones. There was only one large bone forming a cross or T in the middle, and little chance of swallowing it by mistake.

The four sat eating and conversing enjoying each other's company. The meal that had required hours of obtaining, cleaning, and preparation had disappeared in 20 minutes. The only evidence left of the fine meal was the collection of the Barracuda's bones and the butt ends of some of the chilies.

With the body now busy digesting the meal, and a light fog having settled over their faculties from the beer, the conversation of the three men became slower.

Teresa began gathering up the plates and attended to matters in her small kitchen. She tossed the bones out through a window and they sank down into the water. Francisco stretched his back and suggested that they go outside and sit.

As they slowly stood up the sound of the benches dragging on the wood floor echoed inside the house. The two guests expressed their thankfulness for the meal and their admiration for the cook. To her, it was all well worth it just knowing that she was appreciated. Their feet seemed heavier. Their steps were somewhat awkward and made with reluctance. They managed to untangle themselves though from the table and the benches and headed for the door with their host in the lead.

The platform where Francisco's house was built provided for a small area to one side where benches could be placed. The three men picked out spots where they could sit and enjoy the breeze that was coming from the direction of the mainland, still savoring the taste of the coconut oil in their mouths.

"So, what is this help you want from me? The question made Jorge sit up and dispel the heaviness that had fallen on his eyes.

"You still work for the packing plant?"

"Yes."

"Is there a chance to get my friend here on one of the boats as a deck hand and get him to the States?" Jorge knew that the packing plant after processing the lobster and shrimp would send the finished product North. Francisco considered the question.

"I can ask. He will have to work you know." Looking at Bill he questioned him. "You don't mind hard work with a rough lot do you? The guys who work on the ships aren't the most congenial people. Why do you want to ship out on a seafood freighter? It's no vacation." Then after a brief silence he continued.

"You *gringos* are a curious bunch. You know, there was a German who came through here. He had ridden a bicycle from who knows where, through several countries over on the mainland, and then he got out here and shipped out on a boat as a deck hand just like you want to do. He was living off of powdered milk and bananas. He looked healthy enough. What a strange thing, riding a bike and then out to sea. Yeah, you people are wanderers." These comments were interspersed with chuckles, Francisco's voice falling and rising with the different stages of his conversation.

"When can you find out?"

"Tomorrow. When I go in I will ask about it and see if a deck hand is needed. They aren't too reliable. Most of them are alcoholics, drug users. A pretty rough lot like I said. They sign up for work and then don't show up. So, we will see what we can do for you." Jorge slapped his hands on his knees and showed his approval of Francisco's willingness with a nod of the head.

"Good! Tonight we will sleep well knowing that you are looking into the matter."

The subject then changed, Francisco and Jorge each taking turns bringing up matters of interest to them. Bill was pleased that he was called upon only rarely to give his opinion, and then his words were to be brief as Francisco had apparently saved up his commentaries on life and its vicissitudes for some time and was only in need of someone to listen. A nod of the head, a grunt of approval was the only requirements to keep Francisco going.

The years of life, the food and the beer had settled Jorge into a state of restfulness and tranquility, so much so that he caught himself lapsing into a delightful sleep. Each time he approached that point a sudden jump of his leg, or an aborted snore roused him in time to say something that would indicate he was still very much a part of Francisco's monologue. It was such a beautiful part of the day, the twilight over the mainland, the cool air, no pangs of an empty stomach, and the promise of enjoying a good night's rest ahead.

Pauses began to creep into Francisco's review of the day and the events of years gone by, indicating that he as well as his guests were at the point of retiring for the evening. The neighbors began closing the wood shudders of their dwellings and the lights began to appear and disappear inside as the evening came upon them.

It didn't come unexpectedly when he announced that it was time to get things in order for sleeping, and all agreed that it was time to do just that.

The three men rose, rather slowly, stretching and yawning, Bill and Francisco doing so with more vigor than Jorge, as his years did not afford him the energy to be so vigorous at the end of a long day.

Teresa had been busy preparing the two *Tijeras* or cots, portable beds with wood frames and attached canvas that could be opened like a pair of scissors. There was a small pillow on each bed and a sheet. This would be more than adequate for a good night's sleep. The beds, as well as the pillows and sheets were well used but appeared to be clean.

Seeing the preparations his wife had performed Francisco felt all was in order. However, as a gracious host he insisted that his guests make mention of anything they needed.

In regards to the next day it was all quite simple. He would go to work in the morning and as soon as he could he would speak with a supervisor about Bill's desire to sign on as a deck hand. At noon, he would come back to tell them what he had found out.

With these arrangements in place they said their good nights, and the four retired to their respective sides of the room. A wood frame covered with cloth divided the front room into two separate areas. It wasn't long before they were all asleep, oblivious to the hours of the night quietly passing them by.

Chapter 16
Route To The North

Francisco and Teresa were both up and conversing in hushed undertones. Jorge had gotten out of bed because the more he stayed in a prone position the more complaints his body was lodging with him. Bill was somewhere between asleep and awake, listening partially to Francisco as he prepared to leave for work. With all of the movement it was futile to stay in bed any longer. He finally made a supreme effort and sat up on the edge of the cot. His fingers had apparently forgotten how to communicate with the rest of his body and were busy fumbling with the laces of his shoes. When they were sufficiently secured he thought it time to head for the bathroom, wanting to get in as soon as Jorge was out. The facilities were located outside, connected to the house but not accessible from within.

Teresa was in the kitchen. Her husband had told her to have something ready for their guests when they got up. She was preparing some rice and milk in a porridge of sorts, a good deal of sugar and some cinnamon sticks would make it into a warm, sweet mixture to start the day. The people on the island were accustomed to starting their day early to get ahead of the heat as best they could.

When Jorge came back inside Bill now saw it as his opportunity. Arranging his pants and shirt he leaned around the corner of the kitchen to greet Teresa. She seemed pleased with this gesture of interest.

Turning around he almost bounced off of Jorge who was right behind him looking to find a cup of coffee if he could. He greeted him and answered the customary question on how he had slept, but without prolonging the conversation. He knew that his body had reached the limit of endurance, and finding the bathroom was a priority.

Maneuvering his way to the door he stepped out and rounded the corner to where the bathroom was located. The door opened without much trouble and he entered a small room. His head nearly collided twice with a pipe sticking out some seven inches from the wall. This fixture served as the shower.

An individual could tend to all his needed affairs in this one little room with real economy of movement. He realized that when he saw a plank with an appropriately sized hole that was obviously the toilet. A stream of reflected light from the sea below was shimmering up through this opening leaving no doubt as to where the sewage ended up. As he stood there attending to matters he reflected on the Barracuda they had eaten the night before.

"Man, I hope they caught that thing out in deep water."

Having taken care of pressing needs he now felt a great deal more civil. Exiting the bathroom he met up with Jorge who with coffee cup in hand was seeking a place on the bench outside the house.

"Teresa has some coffee if you are in need of a cup."

"Sounds good." His legs were still in the process of coming to grips with the day, a fact he realized when he nearly stumbled, his foot having caught on the planking of the walkway. He bent over to tie his shoes again as the laces had not been tied sufficiently. Returning to a standing position he passed his fingers through his hair bringing some order to the top of his head. As he entered the house the obstacle course of the cots greeted him. He maneuvered around them and went into the kitchen area adjacent to the front room.

"Teresa, pardon me, but Jorge told me that you have some coffee for us."

"I sure do." She took hold of a blue porcelain pot that contained boiling water. It had been heating on the kerosene two-burner stove. The ground coffee was dumped into a funnel shaped cloth attached to a wire frame. She held the funnel over a cup and the dark liquid passed through the cloth as she poured out the coffee.

"There you go. Tell Jorge if he wants more to let me know." He nodded with his head and then raised the cup to his lips and began enjoying the hot brew.

"This is great! Thanks so much." Her smile indicated the pleasure she felt. "Pardon me if I go outside and sit with Jorge."

"No, no problem. Go right ahead. When you two want something to eat I have some rice and milk here for you. Oh, and if you want more sugar for the coffee it is on the table." He acknowledged the kindness and after adding a little more sweetener to the thick black liquid he headed for the door. Passing the cots his eyes sought out his backpack. It was sitting in a corner where he had left it, inviolate as he had hoped.

Jorge had slept well and was in a jovial mood. So much so that he commented on the similarity between a porcupine and his friend' s hair, which on one side had stubbornly refused to lie down and so stood erect like quills. The good-natured remark didn't perturb him, as he knew it to be true. Though he had tried to tame the spot with his fingers.

"Francisco and his wife are really good people." The words came out amongst a yawn and a sip of the coffee.

"They are among the best I have known. Some of the best." There were a few minutes of silence as the two continued the process of beginning the new day. Jorge had a lead on Bill as he had already enjoyed his cup of coffee and felt energized from the sleep and the caffeine. Looking at him he asked,

"So, porcupine, what are we going to do until noon? How about we look over the island after eating some of the rice Teresa has for us." Bill, still convincing himself that he was awake looked in a quasi disbelief at his friend.

"You must be feeling pretty good this morning."

"Yes, I am. Strangely enough for this body." With that he stood up, not too fast, and then he stretched like a cat. "You can finish your coffee inside. Let's go have some of the rice." He had been thinking of it longingly as it was one of his favorite dishes. Bill would have been pleased to sit awhile longer, but he gave in to the coaxing and accompanied his friend into the house where Teresa served each of them a large bowl.

After leisurely eating their fill they were ushered out with much respect and kindness to attend to whatever they needed to do. But, not before being reminded that they were to be back at midday. Francisco would come home and he expected to see them at the noon meal. This reminder was accepted gratefully as two excellent meals had already been enjoyed, and a third one was not to be rejected.

Before they left, Bill shared his concern with Jorge about the backpack, whether it was safe to leave it unattended or not. He was assured that in this house he could leave his precious statue on a table and neither Francisco nor Teresa would touch it. It was out of the way and didn't attract any attention. Being satisfied with the comments he felt more at ease in leaving it in the corner behind a chair where it was out of sight. He agreed to heading out with Jorge on an exploration of the cay.

They wandered along the wood walkways with the sound of their feet being amplified by the boards and the sea beneath them. One of the docked shrimp boats caught the attention of Jorge. There were several men scurrying about repairing or installing some kind of winch, maneuvering it into place and calling out to one another on how to do it without damage to the equipment or harm to themselves. The boat was wide and deep displacing a good deal of water. The space in the hold was necessary as the boats would be out for weeks at a time until they had gathered all the catch they could manage.

The two walked along enjoying an unhurried conversation. Jorge was taking the lead in commenting about life on the island.

Their wanderings brought them to where a large ship was docked. It was a lifeless hulk with no visible activity, a curiosity, a cargo vessel not equipped for fishing. It definitely wasn't a ship used for transporting frozen seafood to the North, obviously being in disrepair and needing maintenance. They were looking it over, Jorge muttering something about its not being a fishing vessel and Bill shaking his head in agreement.

They were a little startled when a voice from behind them suddenly spoke up.

"You want to buy it?" The statement was made by a rugged looking fisherman who had more than a few days of having been in the sun, *cantinas*, and on the wrong side in a fight. Jorge upon looking him over perceived that the comment had been made as a joke.

"No, I don't think my horse could pull it." The comment elicited a raucous laugh from the fisherman. Then the old man asked; "What is it doing here?"

"This ship, my friend, was found adrift with no crew aboard." Jorge raised his eyebrows at the statement. Bill, who was studying the vessel, turned abruptly to look at the man."

"What do you mean no crew?"

"Oh, what do we have here? A *gringo* has come to visit."

Though Bill's Spanish was excellent, he still had an accent identifying him as a foreigner, and he knew better than to allow the comment to wound his pride or to bait him. So, he smiled and followed the current of the conversation.

"Yeah, between my horse and my friends we can probably pull it back home. Are you the owner?" Again, the fisherman let out a bellow.

"You know, I like you two. Tell me, what brings you to this paradise?" With that said he lowered a burlap bag he was carrying on his back, letting out a sigh of relief as it touched the ground.

"We are visiting with an old friend of mine who used to live on the mainland, in San Juan."

"Oh, I see." Then with a bit of sarcasm he added, "San Juan? It is a long way to San Juan. It must be a very important visit you are making. Not too many would travel so far unless they had a very important reason. But, then, who am I to doubt what others tell me." Obviously he was fishing for information. After a brief silence he smiled and tightened his eyes until he looked much like one of the rats that ran amongst the stacks of cargo.

Jorge never let his vision drop from the fisherman, his expression telling the man that he was not one to be intimidated or cowed. The fisherman began to shake his head in a gentle affirmation of what he sensed about the character of Jorge. He was old, but he was a man of solid character. The sinister aspect of the fisherman changed somewhat as he turned his head away to look at the ship.

"Tell me my good friends, do you want to see on board our ship?" Bill was a little apprehensive at hearing the invitation, and Jorge was wary but accepted the opportunity to take up the fisherman on his offer.

"Where do we climb up?"

"Come on I will show you." He then took the lead as if the ship were his own, guiding them to a gangplank hidden partially by old crates. Thick ropes securely fastened the vessel. The sea was gentle on this side of the cay, so there was hardly any movement and the ship so large that it wasn't easily set in motion. They climbed the gangplank.

A military vessel had towed the ship into port from where it was found. If it had continued to drift aimlessly it would have posed a threat to other vessels. An oddity, that is what it was, and it could be visited by any who wished to go aboard.

Sea birds had stained the decks and the machinery as well as any other available place with white, repugnant fishy smelling excrement. The birds were in constant attendance upon the vessel.

The fisherman now became their guide, indicating where the engine room was, the mess hall and kitchen as well as other details unknown to those who have never sailed on a cargo ship. The hold was vacant, and the moans of a terminal illness were made known by the scraping and creaking sounds they heard coming from the steel skin of the ship. Water was sloshing about in the darkness somewhere in the hold below. They climbed a ladder to an upper deck and then walked along the side of the vessel to the bridge where they entered through a heavy steel door that didn't wish to cooperate.

"This is the bridge." Bill looked around and his curiosity continued to grow. He saw books, some garments, papers and other items that would have been of daily use to the sailors. The items were strewn about the floor and the consoles, indicating that the ship had been abandoned in haste.

"Why would the crew just abandon a ship like this at sea? Is there any damage anywhere, or was it taking on water?" The fisherman smiled at the questions.

"Good questions my foreign friend. What do you think? Was there a storm? Was it pirates? Or, was the ship carrying something valuable? And when that cargo was off-loaded to smaller vessels at sea, was it time to abandon the ship before anyone could find out what had taken place?" The manner in which he expressed the last option indicated that he knew more about the reason why it was set adrift then he was willing to admit. Jorge felt it best not to ask more questions or to hear more details on the matter. He suggested that it was time to move on.

When they had reached the main deck leading to the gangplank Bill heard the noise of an approaching plane. He raised his eyes to the sky. Shielding his face with his hands he could see an approaching DC-3. They made one trip to the island each week. But, this one was unscheduled, and it was a military plane not the usual passenger flight. It flew over their heads as it made its approach to the landing strip located on the other side of the waterway separating the island from the cay. The noise lessened and it disappeared behind some buildings.

Their guide unconcerned with the plane conducted them to the bottom of the gangplank.

"How long will you fine gentlemen be staying?" Jorge raised his hat a little above his brow, and then smiled at the fisherman before answering.

"Until we return to San Juan." That answer said a great deal to the fisherman about Jorge. In a spirit of respect and with some seriousness in his voice he replied.

"Well then, may God be with you in your journey my friend." The two began to walk away, and the fisherman stood watching them before he disappeared as fast as he had appeared.

"He was a strange individual. It seemed like he knew more about the ship than he was willing to say." Jorge stopped walking and looked at Bill.

"Sometimes it is best to know when you should know nothing." The younger man thought about the statement briefly, and then indicated his agreement with the counsel by a nod of his head.

Their wanderings on the cay kept them occupied and completely unaware of what was taking place at the landing strip. The DC-3 that had arrived was carrying

Colonel Guzmán and a group of eight soldiers. Another passenger, a civilian was on board, it was Nicolás. The Colonel and Nicolás had been busy talking to people, asking questions and demanding answers. They were sufficiently informed to know that the foreigner had found something of value and was trying to take a back door out of the country.

Jorge didn't know that his young daughter, overcome by curiosity, had opened the backpack at the house and found the statue inside. She told her mother what she had found. From there Reina had spoken with a neighbor lady, and that woman had added a few of her own thoughts to the tale before passing it on to other neighbors. The result was that several knew that the foreigner was after some artifact worth a great deal of money.

The Colonel and Nicolás had found the way to inform themselves through questions and intimidation. It wasn't to mine gold or silver that had attracted the foreigner to the falls that day. He had retrieved an artifact of immense worth. Now, it was up to them to take it from him, and as loyal citizens benefit themselves from his find.

The Colonel had notified the local commander, Sergeant Ávila that he was to meet the plane at the landing strip, and the Sergeant was in route from the cay to the island. The sudden visit of the Colonel had perturbed the peaceful existence of the Sergeant, who was now rubbing his face nervously trying to guess what the nature of the visit was. His words were few and direct to the soldier with him.

"Bring it around, bring it around! That's it, far enough. Tie it up." His orders were immediately obeyed and the rope was passed securely over the posts on the wharf.

"Well, let's go see what the old man wants." He stood as straight as his paunch would allow him, trying to tuck in his shirt as he walked and straightening his belt and the holster where he carried a 38-caliber pistol. His apprehension grew as he saw the Colonel exiting the plane, accompanied by a contingent of overly armed soldiers dressed in camouflaged uniforms and flack jackets.

The Colonel, his sunglasses overshadowing his face, stood waiting for the Sergeant. The permanent scowl he wore was especially grim, not at all softened by his protruding lips and puffy jowls.

"Colonel Guzmán." The Sergeant stiffened and saluted as he greeted his superior. The salute was returned but in a perfunctory and casual manner.

Adding a note of comedy to the solemnity of the visit was Nicolás. He was trying to exit the plane and almost succeeded in falling in a perfect landing on his face. The accompanying soldiers knew better than to be distracted by the one-man show. They were attentive, with their weapons pointing towards the ground in a ready but non-threatening posture.

"The visit is a surprise, but a welcome one Sir." The Colonel knew better than to believe the statement. The Sergeant discretely wiped away his sweat. He wasn't sure yet if his superior had found out about the lucrative bribes he was receiving as commander of the island. The Colonel knew about the bribes, but he wasn't worried about them because the ones he received were even bigger.

"Sergeant, yesterday an old man and a *gringo* came out here traveling from the mainland in a dory. Do you know where they are?" The Sergeant's relief was obvious when he heard the question. Now he knew that the visit wasn't to sack him and haul him off to the brig.

"Yes Sir, they are here. According to my sources they are staying with a welder who lives on the cay."

"Good. You have six men under your command here on the island, don't you?"

"Yes, Sir."

"Take your men and find the two I mentioned, and bring them to me." He added as an afterthought, "Bring them with any personal items they have, backpacks, bags, whatever. Do it without any force if possible, but, bring them." The Colonel saluted but now with an air of professionalism and authority.

The Sergeant and one of his men, the one that had accompanied him out to the landing strip, moved with haste back to their boat.

"You heard what he said, he wants the old man and the *gringo*. When we get back I want you to find García, Méndez and the rest of the guys and tell them to come to the shack." The Sergeant in everyday conversation with his men addressed them as members of his personal company, dropping all military formality. He had found it beneficial to treat them as business partners. The "shack" was his office.

Jorge and Bill had tired of their excursion. They were thinking of heading back to Francisco's to meet him as they had agreed at noon. They came around a corner of a building on the main part of the cay and almost ran head on with two soldiers of the security force. They were coming in the opposite direction, and obviously were wasting no time in getting to the *Comandancia*.

"Whoa! Sorry about that. Pardon us." The soldiers were unaware of why the Sergeant wanted them at the office in such a hurry. They were wasting no time and no words with these two strangers that they had collided with.

"Excuse us." With military precision they continued on their way.

"They were sure in a hurry."

"It is getting close to noon, they are late to eat." Jorge was still feeling energetic enough to enjoy lighter moments. He then thought about his own stomach.

"What will Teresa have for us today? Whatever it is it will be good. She is a good cook you know." Thinking of his own wife he added in her defense; "Almost as good as my Reina back home."

As they neared Francisco's house some children came towards them. They were running excitedly and at the same time trying to catch a glimpse of something that was coming from behind. Jorge and Bill couldn't see what was around the corner on the walkway. Then the soldiers came into view. The soldiers were prodding Francisco along, who apparently wasn't very pleased, nor was he in a cooperative mood.

Some of the local women upon hearing the commotion stuck their heads out to see what was taking place. When they saw the soldiers they immediately understood that something was afoot. It was time to tell their children to get in the house before shots were fired.

When the soldiers caught sight of Bill and Jorge they took hold of their weapons in a more aggressive manner. One of them called out for the two to stop where they were. There was little else that they could do, so, the two stood motionless awaiting what was about to take place. Upon reaching them the soldiers took up positions cutting off any chance of fleeing, which the two had not considered. Jorge looked at his friend and inquired what was happening.

"Francisco, what is this? Are you in trouble?" He said nothing, but shook his head. His expression indicated a good deal of disdain for the treatment he was receiving, and concern for his friends from the mainland. The same soldier who had called out for them to halt directed himself to the pair.

"You are being detained. Come with us."

"And, can we ask why we are being detained?" There was disbelief in Bill's voice at what was happening. The answer he received was curt, cold, and emotionless.

"No, you cannot. Come along!" The other soldiers, acting on a gesture of the one taking the lead, prodded the two with their rifles encouraging them along. Bill noticed that one of the soldiers was carrying his backpack as well as the other items they had left in Francisco's house.

"What about the welder?"

"Our orders said the two. Let him go." The soldier who was restraining Francisco let go of his arm. Jorge looked at his friend and managed a muted smile. He was comforted by his release. In their case there were no options open to them, other than complying with this show of force.

Retrieving their goods from Francisco's house, finding them and the march to the boat was accomplished in a short time, and without a struggle. However, the action didn't take place without notice by some of the neighbors, who were already busy in broadcasting the matter through the local gossip channels. Some watched cautiously from areas hidden from view. Others, feeling that no gunplay was involved came out of their houses and watched as if a parade were passing, commenting quietly when once the group had passed.

They were taken to one of the docks where the Sergeant with nervous expectancy was waiting. He had one foot placed on the side of the boat resting his weight on that leg. When he caught sight of the group coming towards him he withdrew his foot, standing erect. He took hold of his belt, weighed down by everything he had attached to it and yanked upward. His pants had developed an uncooperative habit of falling to lower areas.

The two prisoners were pushed on board. Four soldiers followed them, all the while keeping them at gunpoint. The engine was started, the lines withdrawn from the pier and soon the wake behind the boat widened out over the water as they headed rapidly for the main island and the landing strip.

Chapter 17
The Final Reward

T he process of exiting the boat was similar to what had taken place on the other side at the cay. Only now they were exiting rather than boarding the vessel.

They came up alongside the dock, the boat was tied securely in place, and the two detainees were taken out in a rather rough manner. The Sergeant of course took the lead, knowing that the Colonel would be waiting. It would be in his best interests to be seen in front. Jorge and Bill were not sure of what was taking place. Were they being flown back to the mainland? Why would they be going to the landing strip if it were otherwise?

The Colonel, Nicolás, and the soldiers that came with them were in the shade of an awning that spanned the length of the airline office. Though calling it an office was a positive assessment, as it was little more than a wood shack furnished with two tables and folding chairs for some 20 persons. The Colonel had his hands folded behind his back surveying the approach of the Sergeant and his retinue. He was rocking back and forth on his feet, obviously enjoying the moment. Nicolás, with a sheepish look was considering how he was going to face Jorge. For once in his life he actually was feeling ambivalence about his actions. The Colonel moved out from underneath the awning, his men reacting quickly to this movement forming their detachment behind him.

"Colonel. Here are the two you requested." With an obsequious salute the Sergeant greeted him. The Colonel managed a half smile.

"Well done! You and your men can return to the boat now. My men and I will handle matters. But don't leave for the cay until I give you the order." They saluted each other and the Sergeant with much pleasure to be off of the radar screen ordered his men back to the boat. Before he could leave there was another detail that needed attention.

"Sergeant, do you have the personal belongings of these two?"

"Yes, I do Sir." He had almost forgotten the items. "Private Jiménez, give the backpack and the bags to the Colonel." They were deposited on a table near the Colonel.

"My men and I will wait by the boat, Sir." He turned and with his men walked in the direction of the landing.

Jorge said nothing. His eyes however spoke volumes. Nicolás still could not look at him, so Jorge finally spoke up.

"Nicolás. What a surprise to see you here. And, why are you accompanying the good Colonel?" There was much the old man wished to say to him but he knew that it was not the time for such words. He could guess that if Nicolás was involved there was nothing good to be gained from this affair.

The soldiers accompanying the Colonel took up positions to maintain control of the two detainees. The Colonel walked over to Jorge, strutting somewhat like a proud rooster. Seeing that they were about the same height he cast a look of indifference and disgust at Jorge. But, Bill being much taller than the Colonel was another story. When the Colonel stood in front of him he could see the disparity in their height. The difference was a little discomforting to his pride, so he quickly moved back to a neutral position in front of the two.

"I understand that you have something of value which you are trying to get out of the country." He wasted no time in coming to the main point for his visit.

"As the military representative of the government, I should inform you that what you have done is illegal." As of yet he had not searched through the belongings that lay on the table. He was convinced that what he had been told about the activity of the two and the tale of the statue was a certainty.

"Do you wish to tell me where the item is?" Bill could see that there was no reason to continue with their plan. At this point, cooperation might lessen the sting of defeat and the punishment that hung over them.

"It's in the backpack." The Colonel looked at him.

"You are wise to cooperate." He walked over to the table and took hold of the backpack setting it upright. He again looked at Bill and then began pulling out clothing, note pads and other items. When his fingers came in contact with a solid item he momentarily ran his fingers along it. His blood pressure increased betrayed by a purplish-red hue that came over his face. Almost forgetting himself and those who stood around him he feverishly pulled the object from the bag. The afternoon sun reflected off of the gold, shimmering brilliantly. For a moment not just the Colonel, but Nicolás and the soldiers were taken back by the treasure that they had before them. No one spoke as the Colonel moved the statue in his hands considering the idol from different angles before he laid it carefully on the table.

"In the name of the Sovereign Republic I am seizing this item and placing you two under arrest." He then barked out an order. "Place the handcuffs on them."

Bill looked at Jorge, what could be said. There was little that could be said at this point.

"I am sorry for getting you in this situation." Nothing was said in reply.

"Nicolás, come with me." The Colonel took him to one side and then discussed the situation with him. They knew that Jorge and Bill could say nothing about what was taking place. Why would they implicate themselves in an illegal affair? They could do nothing to the Colonel, and how would they incriminate Nicolás? They could be held for three days, sufficient time for the Colonel and Nicolás to accomplish what they needed to do, turn the statue into hard cash. Then, they could be set free. The foreigner would go back to the States and Jorge to San Juan. That would be the end of the matter. Nothing else was needed.

They talked animatedly for some time before returning to the group. The Colonel then directed himself to one of the soldiers.

"Tell the Sergeant I want to speak with him."

"Yes, Sir." With alacrity he moved off towards the landing and soon came back with the Sergeant, who was out of breath at this hurried order to return.

"Sergeant, come with me." He took him out of listening range of the group.

"You are to take these two men back to the *Comandancia*. Lock them up for three days and then, you can let them go, not before. Those are your orders, do you understand." Though he understood them he wasn't sure of what was taking place, but he knew that it was best to follow explicitly what he was told.

"Yes, Sir. Three days it will be Sir. Are there charges, Sir?"

"No charges. Put them in protective custody for three days." Again there was the exchange of salutes, purely formal, as there was no mutual respect between the two.

The Sergeant called his men back and instructed them to take charge of the prisoners.

Jorge and Bill were bewildered with all of this movement. They were again prodded with the rifles to walk towards the boat, which they did, and this time handcuffed.

The Colonel and his men, along with Nicolás who followed obediently like a trained puppy, climbed back on board the plane. However, before they boarded the statue was wrapped in a cloth, and then placed securely in an attaché case that had been brought precisely for this purpose.

When the Sergeant and his prisoners arrived on the cay there were several men who were sitting there waiting for the results of this military activity. After all, a little excitement of this nature was cheap entertainment. They watched as the two prisoners were alternately pulled and shoved from the boat and then marched off to the *Comandancia*.

Francisco out of concern for his friend was already informing himself of what had taken place. He felt that if the two were detained on the cay then there was hope that this would not come to a bad end. Had they gone back to the mainland in the plane it would be doubtful if he would ever see Jorge or the foreigner again.

The Sergeant seemed almost gleeful that this sudden visit of the Colonel had come to its end, and apparently, he still had his profitable and comfortable assignment.

He even became a bit more civil towards his detainees. He was familiar with how things were handled in the area, and the fact that the two were left alive and were to be set free in three days, not even any charges being leveled, well then, the problem must have been of a personal nature, something between the two and the Colonel. So, why be rough on them. The group arrived back in the *Comandancia* and the Sergeant gave orders to take the handcuffs off.

"Listen to me, both of you. You could be fish bait by now. But, you are getting off. I don't know what happened between you and the Colonel, but it is over, so be happy." He paused in his comments briefly.

"I am to hold you for three days and then let you go. So don't make trouble for me and things will be fine. Is that understood?" Jorge lifted his head and opened his eyes wider when he heard the Sergeant's words. He looked at Bill before addressing the Sergeant.

"You are to hold us for three days? Then what?"

"I told you. You are getting out of here old man. My counsel would be to get back in a dory and head for San Juan forgetting whatever you two were up to. Listen to me. I am not an unreasonable person. I am happy with my life and I don't want anyone making trouble for me. Just sit down and take it easy for three days, don't make my life miserable." He then spoke with one of the soldiers.

"Take both of them to the holder and lock them in. And, don't be rough on them. "The order had scarcely been made when Francisco stepped in from the street. The Sergeant turned to face him.

"Francisco! My friend, I don't want any problems with you either. I don't know how you are mixed up in this deal, or even if you are. But, your buddies here had a run in with the Colonel and they are going to have a free room for three days." Francisco looked at him with a perplexed expression.

"What do you mean three days, Sergeant?"

"They are my guests here in the *Comandancia* for three days, and then I am setting them free." As he was speaking he was busy opening the drawers of his desk, looking for something. He took off his hat and put it on the desk, scratching his head.

"Francisco, I don't want you holding any of this against me, you and I have always gotten along well. I do what I am told and that is why I keep this assignment, so, no hard feelings, o.k. I know my boys were a little rough on you. But, hey, these things happen."

"Three days? There won't be any fine, nothing?" The Sergeant stopped his activity and looked at Francisco in a fixed gaze.

"No fine, no jail, they walk out of here in three days. And you had better convince them to go back to San Juan and forget all of this."

Francisco had lived amongst the islanders long enough to know something about the Sergeant. He was dishonest, involved in contraband, took bribes and he caused his share of scandals. Yet, he had a side to him that was likable. As long as he didn't come out loosing he was willing to tell the truth and let others have their place in the sun.

Francisco looked at Jorge.

"Don't worry. If that is what the Sergeant says, I believe him. Just sit tight for the three days." He turned to the Sergeant again.

"Can I bring them some food?" Francisco knew that the food provided in the *Comandancia* was minimal and basically unpalatable.

"Yeah." He said loudly with an agreeable laugh. "And bring me some too." With the talk of food a thought came to the Sergeant. It was about time for a cup of coffee, and he made known his desire to one of the soldiers.

Francisco called out to Jorge and Bill who were being taken to the holding cell, telling them that he would return later with something for them to eat.

There was no pushing or cajoling by the soldiers this time, they only pointed the way and showed some confidence in the reliability and peacefulness of the two. There was a large, heavy wood frame door with steel bars that the soldier opened. The two stepped in and the door was closed behind them.

It was no luxury hotel. There were eight wood bunks with something that looked like a blanket on each. The only light was that which came in through the small windows, three on each side up near the ceiling. A bucket sitting in a corner was no doubt the latrine. On a shelf there was another bucket half full of water, possibly for washing but definitely not for drinking. A few cockroaches scurried to darker areas of the holding pen and the smell of mold clouded the air. This was to be their home for three days.

Bill moved one of the blankets to one side of a bottom bunk and when he was reasonably sure that no bugs were crawling about he sat down. He placed his hands over his face and let out a deep and drawn out puff of air.

"This is not quite the way I envisioned everything. I lost the chance of a lifetime."

Jorge with more years and experience to his credit considered the statement.

"You have your life my young friend. In three days we will leave with our life. That is worth more than the statue." Bill absorbed the meaning of those words and he slowly began to appreciate the reality of what they meant. He had his life.

They sat there for a moment without saying anything while in the distance the engines of the DC-3 came to life.

The Colonel and his group were heading back to the mainland. It was a short flight to span the thirty miles that separated the island from the mainland, and it would pass even more rapidly as the haughty giddiness that the Colonel and Nicolás were feeling didn't allow them any negative attitude. The expectancy of the riches to be gained dwarfed any feelings of remorse or misgivings.

The pilot brought the plane around, revving the engines and kicking up dust scattering some of the dry vegetation lying on the dirt runway. Everyone was strapped in. Nicolás and the Colonel fought a momentary battle with the seat belt to convince it that it could span their girth. With some reluctance the buckle finally clicked shut and they managed to get a breath of air despite the restriction. The plane began its take off gathering speed and slowly lifting into the air. It banked to the left and those on board could see out the windows the multicolored waters sparkling, turquoise, blue, green, deep blue, the colors marking the end of the coral and the beginning of the depths. What a beautiful site. There was no need to gain a great deal of altitude; the flight would end almost as rapidly as it began. Looking towards the flight deck, as there was no door, the mainland could be seen through the forward windows. The movement of the plane in the cross winds was detected by the sliding of the panorama before them from side to side.

The Colonel looked down at his feet. Next to his laced boots was the attaché case. Inside it was an article that would bring him a good deal of money after paying out a small percentage to Nicolás. He smiled and thought happily of the inability of Nicolás to make any complaint of the percentage he would receive.

Back on the cay, Francisco had Teresa prepare some food that he could take to the *Comandancia*. She had carefully placed the scrambled eggs, beans, and fried plantains in a metal pan with divided compartments. Some tortillas wrapped in a towel were warm and fresh and the smell of the corn enlivened the appetite.

As he carried the food to the *Comandancia* he was just about to the door when a bright flash to his left caught his eye, and then the sound of a dull thud like an explosion. He looked towards the sky and saw in the distance some dark objects, pieces of a DC-3, the Colonels DC-3. One of the engines had exploded and a wing had separated from the fuselage. It was spiraling downward. It hit the water in a definitive final act. Several of the neighbors had come out of their houses and were asking what had happened, some knew, some didn't. The Sergeant had heard the explosion and came running out of the *Comandancia*, looking in the direction of where the plane had been. With a degree of solemnity he spoke to Francisco who was standing with the food in his hand.

"It was the Colonel's plane." He stood stunned for a moment, and then rapidly ran inside where he began issuing orders to get the boats to the zone as fast as possible. His men jumped and ran to notify the boat masters of the accident and the need to get to the site of where it went down.

Francisco stood with the food in his hand, a state of disbelief weighing on him. Around him people were talking, others running towards the boats. Dazed, he turned and headed back home to inform his wife.

The Sergeant was able to gather some of the faster sport fishing boats. He convinced their owners that it was in their own best interests to cooperate in searching for survivors. Sometimes it takes tragic circumstances to prompt men to do what they should. In this case, the camaraderie of those who venture on the sea brought out the community spirit in them. All of them knew that possibly the boats might be looking for them someday.

When they arrived at the site where the plane went down there was little to be seen. Some oil and fuel on the surface, a minimal amount of floating debris. The boats circled around, cutting their engines back, listening, and looking. No sign of survivors. The plane had broken up and slipped into the sea before anyone could escape.

Though not far from the island the reefs had disappeared completely, and the bottom was almost six hundred feet below the circling boats. They began to accept the reality that the Colonel, the pilots, the soldiers and Nicolás were not to be seen again

The plane had sunk rapidly, coming to rest on the bottom. The wreckage momentarily displaced the sand in plumes that floated back down on what was left of the plane in a symbolic burial.

Chapter 18
A Lesson Learned

T he boats returned to harbor with no lack of individuals waiting for news on what had taken place. Why did the plane go down, and who was on it? Were there survivors?

Within minutes it became apparent that no one had escaped. The sullen expressions of those returning indicated that the effort had been fruitless. Those who participated in the attempted rescue, as well as the ones who were waiting on the docks, were quiet, subdued. All but the very young were pensive. They knew that a similar end could await them. The sea could easily claim any one of them someday.

From their cell Jorge and Bill could hear the commotion outside. They also were able to hear some of the comments that were being made by those who passed the *Comandancia*. The conversations were disjointed, and at times not totally understood. They heard sufficient to glean from what was being said to know that a plane had gone down. When they finally realized what was taking place they looked at each other, saying nothing, and then Bill tried to position himself nearer the small windows to hear more from those outside.

"Do you think it was the Colonel?" Bill spoke in a hushed tone.

"I don't know. But, it must have been his plane. There weren't any others at the landing strip."

There was no feeling of elation on Jorge's part, as if retribution or vengeance had been carried out, both the Colonel and Nicolás meeting an appropriate end. He was old enough and sufficiently experienced in life to understand the foolishness of having such petty sentiments. Though he despised the self centered and corrupt nature of Nicolás, he truly wished him no harm. Thinking of the soldiers who accompanied the Colonel and the pilots, he said somberly:

"The poor souls. I hope it was over quickly for them."

The door of the *Comandancia* opened. The Sergeant and two of his soldiers stepped in continuing a conversation they were engaged in while walking back from the wharf. He told one of them to get him a beer. Taking off his belt he wrapped it around his holster before placing it on the desk and then dropped unceremoniously into his chair.

There was a long pause. Then looking up he said; "Well, I better get it over with."

He reached for the microphone of the communications equipment on his desk and contacted the commanding officer at the battalion headquarters on the mainland. The officer in charge during the Colonel's absence was told what had taken place, with added details for the Sergeant's benefit. Yes, despite his unsparing efforts and his immediate response, no survivors were found. No harm would be done by speaking so well of himself.

In their cell from the back of the *Comandancia* Jorge and Bill could hear clearly the Sergeant's report to his superior.

"It was the Colonel's plane. He and Nicolás, the soldiers, they are dead, all of them, they all went to the bottom." Both of them sat on the edge of the bunks, thinking on what had taken place in the last few hours.

The Sergeant having finished his communication to the mainland placed his feet on his desk and was slowly drinking his beer. His mind was now occupied not so much with the accident, rather, with who would be replacing the Colonel as commanding officer. A change in command could affect him as well if the wrong person would be chosen.

From the back room where the cell was located Jorge coughed loud enough so that it caught the Sergeant's attention. He looked in the direction of the source, pausing, obviously thinking. Withdrawing his feet from the desk he stood and opened a drawer of the desk, from which he pulled out a ring of keys. He walked slowly, twirling the keys somewhat nervously in his hand, and then stood in front of the cell. When Jorge and Bill saw him they stood and moved towards the bars separating them from the Sergeant. Jorge spoke first.

"It was the Colonel's plane, wasn't it?"

"Yes, it was old man, and the Colonel and everybody else went down to the bottom with it." The Sergeant studied his face to see if there was a flicker of satisfaction knowing that the man who had him arrested was gone. There was none. He stood silently for a moment and then inserted a key into the cell door.

"For good behavior I am freeing you two early." They said nothing standing immobile, somewhat dumbfounded. The Sergeant stepped to one side and made a sweeping gesture with his hand bowing slightly.

"I said you two are out of here. Go on home." The ex-prisoners looked at each other and then shuffled out.

Jorge paused, looked at the Sergeant, and then holding eye contact briefly with him, nodded his head.

There was more than one quizzical stare from the locals as Jorge and Bill passed them. Having been detained, then whisked away to the Colonel's presence at the airstrip, arrested and thrown in the local jail, the plane going down with all on board, these details were known to all. Now, here the two men were walking away free. All of this would fuel the local gossip for some time to come.

Francisco was at home. He and Teresa were sitting in the shade on a bench outside their house. It was the wife who nudged her husband's elbow and pointed at the two walking towards them. He immediately stood and headed towards Jorge and Bill obviously elated at seeing them, but somewhat bewildered in how they were no longer detained. There was a strong embrace of friendship and a satisfaction of spirit in knowing that they obviously had been set free.

The rest of the day was passed talking and giving thought to all that had taken place, as well as making arrangements to head back to San Juan in the dory. As the entire affair was over, Bill saw no reason to not relate all the details of his visit. Francisco and his wife sat listening in amazement.

All of them passed the night in restless sleep. Their minds refused to recognize the curfew of the darkness. Nor did their thoughts allow them to forget what could have been, or what could have happened. Each one tossed and rolled trying to sleep. While in the privacy of their own judgments on what had transpired, they waited until the early light of dawn began to announce the new day.

Francisco was the first to get up and begin putting matters in order for sending his guests on their way. Some food was prepared for the daylong trip, good-byes were shared, not knowing when they would see one another again, and then they were escorted to the wharf.

Omar was waiting having readied his dory for the trip, and extremely gratified that after all that had transpired he had two famous passengers traveling with him. He had heard the details of the previous day's proceedings over the last few drinks he was sharing with his acquaintances.

As the sun began its ascent over the sea they were in the dory, heading past the reef and into open waters. Before them in the distance was the mainland. It would be some hours before reaching it.

The day held the promise of being idyllic, the sea calm, the sky clear with a light breeze and the uncertainty of what awaited them was past.

True, Bill had lost out on the riches that he hoped for. But, he could have lost more. How much value would the statue have held for him if all of this had cost him his life? He recalled Jorge's words. "You have your life."

With the motor making its rhythmic sound he reflected not so much on the loss of the statue, rather on his own conduct, and how it put in jeopardy his well being, that of Jorge, Francisco, their wives and the children. He also thought of those who had died. Was the statue worth all that had happened?

Jorge of course was oblivious to the thoughts of his visitor, being more occupied with his own. How thankful he would be to enjoy the company and tranquility of his simple life, of his family.

The dory pushed aside the waters as it plowed through the sea powered by the lawnmower engine. Below them, in the darkness, lay the wreckage of a DC-3, now the unadorned tomb of unfortunate individuals.

On the sea floor amongst the wreckage was an attaché case. Inside was a gold statue, lifeless, cold and of no value to any who had possessed it.

THE END